D1035972

MENDOTA
DATE DUE
MENDOTA
DATE DUE
2 15 03

A STRANGER IN STIRRUP

Sage Hampton rode into Eden Valley with a faint premonition of trouble ahead; before he reached the little cow town of Stirrup, the premonition had given way to a chilling certainty. For he learned that his brother Ross, owner of the Flying H Ranch, had been killed two days before.

Now, he would have to stay and bring Ross's murderer to justice . . .

A STRANGER IN STIRRUP

Wayne C. Lee

First published by Jenkins

This hardback edition 2002
by Chivers Press
by arrangement with
Golden West Literary Agency

ISBN 0 7540 8188 5

British Library Cataloguing in Publication Data available.

Printed and bound in Great Britain by
Bookcraft, Midsomer Norton, Somerset

Wayne C. Lee was born to pioneering homesteaders near Lamar, Nebraska. His parents were old when he was born and it was an unwritten law since the days of the frontier that it was expected that the youngest child would care for the parents in old age. Having grown up reading novels by Zane Grey and William MacLeod Raine, Lee wanted to write Western stories himself. His best teachers were his parents. They might not be able to remember what happened last week by the time Lee had reached his majority, but they shared with him their very clear memories of the pioneer days. In fact they talked so much about that period that it sometimes seemed to Lee he had lived through it himself. Lee wrote a short story and let his mother read it. She encouraged him to submit it to a magazine and said she would pay the postage. It was accepted and appeared as *Death Waits at Paradise Pass* in *Lariat Story Magazine*. In the many Western novels that he has written since, violence has never been his primary focus, no matter what title a publisher might give one of his stories, but rather the interrelationships between the characters and within their communities. These are the dominant characteristics in all of Lee's Western fiction and create the ambiance so memorable in such diverse narratives as *The Gun Tamer* (1963), *Petticoat Wagon Train* (1972), and *Arikaree War Cry* (1992). In the truest sense Wayne C. Lee's Western fiction is an outgrowth of his impulse to create imaginary social fabrics on the frontier and his stories are intended primarily to entertain a reader at the same time as to articulate what it was about these pioneering men and women that makes them so unique and intriguing to later generations. His pacing, graceful style, natural sense of humor, and the genuine liking he feels toward the majority of his characters, combined with a commitment to the reality and power of romance between men and women as a decisive factor in making it possible for them to have a better life together than they could ever hope to have apart, are what most distinguish his contributions to the Western story. His latest novel is *Edge of Nowhere* (1996).

A STRANGER IN STIRRUP

I

Sage Hampton rode into Eden Valley with no more than a faint nagging premonition of trouble ahead. But before he reached the hub of the valley, the little cow town of Stirrup, that premonition had given way to a chilling certainty.

About a mile from town he met a man and slowed his horse, showing an inclination to pass the time of day. The other rider obligingly reined up, lifting his hat and running a gnarled hand over his bald head. His beady black eyes bored into Sage.

"Howdy, stranger," he said.

"Howdy." Sage shifted his long, six-foot-one-inch frame in the saddle and ran his gray eyes over the other man. "Pretty hot today."

"It's always hot in this part of Nebraska in July. Heading any place in particular?"

Sage shook his head slowly. Maybe it was only natural that the man should show such keen interest in a stranger, but, remembering his brother's letters, Sage decided to play it close to the vest.

"A friend of mine settled somewhere in this country. Thought I might drop in on him. Fellow by the name of Ross Hampton."

The bald man rubbed his chin with a knotted fist and stared intently at Sage. "Did you say you were a friend of Ross Hampton?"

Sage's eyebrows pulled together. "That's what I said."

"You're a little late to see Hampton," the other man said slowly. "They had his funeral two days ago."

An icy chill stabbed through Sage. Ross's letters had suggested that there was trouble afoot, but nothing in them had prepared him for a blow like this.

"What happened?" he asked when he was sure of his voice again.

"Better ask whoever killed him," the man said uneasily.

Sage's lips drew tight against his teeth. "Do they kill people without a reason here?"

"There are three or four people who could give good reasons for killing Hampton, but there's no proof that any of them did."

"Who had the reasons?"

The man lifted his hat and ran his hand over his bald pate again. "Reckon I've talked enough," he said. "I'll give you a mite of advice, stranger. Take it for what it's worth. Hampton was your friend, but I wouldn't take that friendship too much to heart."

He lifted the reins on his horse and galloped down the trail. Sage watched him out of sight. It wasn't hard to see what the man meant. To dig into the murder of Ross Hampton would make Sage a marked man. But what the man didn't suspect was the brotherly tie between Sage and the murdered man. Ross had been twelve years older than Sage and in many ways a stranger to him. But he was a brother, and to Sage that was a tie that couldn't be broken.

Of late Ross had been writing earnestly to Sage, trying to persuade him to come to Western Nebraska to help him in the biggest project he had ever dreamed up. At last Sage had given in and come. But now that he was here he was too late.

He nudged his horse on toward the town a mile away. He had come here either to help his brother in his fantastic irrigation project or to talk him out of the idea. Now he would have to stay and bring his murderer to justice. The thought that he might turn back and let the whole thing drop never entered his mind. A Hampton never ran away from a job. And this was a job only a Hampton could do.

He thought of the irrigation project Ross had outlined in his letters. According to Ross's description, his ranch, the Flying H, was up west close to the head of the little spring-fed creek, and there was a place there where the bluffs were close enough together so that a dam could be easily built. Below the Flying H to the south of the creek the bluff fell far back, leaving a level plain several miles long and from one to two miles wide. Rich soil, Ross had said, needing only water to make it a Garden of Eden.

In one letter he had mentioned a party of homesteaders who were going to file on the land. They would pay him for the water his irrigation dam and ditches would supply. It was a bonanza, according to Ross.

Looking over the plain to the south of town, Sage had to agree that it probably would be a farmer's paradise if water could be gotten to it. But Sage was a saddle man. Sodbusters were of little interest to him.

The man he had met was a saddle man, too. Very likely it was among such men that Sage would have to look to find Ross's murderer. Ranchers wouldn't allow a dam to go in upstream and cut off their water, much less bring in homesteaders who would tear up their best grass.

As he reined into the single street of Stirrup, he relaid his plans. He wouldn't be going directly to the Flying H now. In fact, it would be just as well if no one knew he had any connection with Ross Hampton. That would mean a change of name, but that caused him only a second's thought.

As a youngster he had had many fights with older, bigger boys who called him Sagebrush. His father had named him Sage after the sage-covered hills in which he had been born, but he had hated the name. Later he had found it convenient. More than once he had passed under the name of Jim Sage.

The town was bigger than he had expected it to be. Glancing down the long narrow street, he saw two grocery stores, a hotel, two drugstores, a livery barn at the far end, a blacksmith shop and several smaller stores and offices. If there was trouble brewing on the range between cattlemen and settlers, this would be the place to find out about it.

This was a cattle town, catering to cattlemen. It took only one look to tell Sage that. But homesteading meant a lot more people and more trade. Many businessmen would be considering that and would be ready to jump to the settlers when and if the signs looked right.

Sage let his horse drift down the street, noting the unpainted false fronts of the stores beginning to crack from the beating of cold and heat and hard winds that drove the sand with the fury of a shotgun blast. The fine sandy dust in the street was deep and dry. There had been no rain on the range for some time, Sage decided.

He pulled in at the worn hitchrack of a grocery store, started to dismount, then checked himself. That other grocery store down the street was a newer building, and the hitchrack showed that it had been there only a short time. He sat in his saddle another minute and studied the town. One of the drugstores was an old building but it showed signs of having just been brought to life after a long sleep. Slowly it began to make sense to Sage. Here was a town that was really two towns, each section serving its own clientele. And the answer was obvious. The homesteaders Ross had mentioned had already arrived.

He dismounted. This was the old grocery, so it would cater to the rancher trade. He belonged here. A saddle man wouldn't be welcome in the new store.

He crossed the porch, noticing the little drift of sand that had piled up just inside the screen door.

There were half a dozen people in the store, but it was as still as if it were empty. Eyes focused on him, some curious, some filled with veiled hostility. Sage read the signs; he had seen them too often to misunderstand. There was trouble in the air, and every man was expected to state his business quickly. And Sage was stating nothing.

He sauntered down one counter, looking over the things under the glass and on the shelves behind. But what he wanted wasn't going to be easy to get. Information would have a mighty high price tag.

"Something I can do for you?" the clerk asked, coming over to the counter where Sage stood. He was a tall spare man with a hooked nose and sharp penetrating eyes. His receding hairline made his face look overly long.

"Just killing a little time waiting for it to cool off," he said.

"Riding through?"

"Riding, anyway," Sage said.

He noticed the shifting feet over against the other counter and the exchange of glances.

"Any place in particular?" the clerk insisted.

"A man doesn't ride in this weather just for the fun of it," Sage said, irritation kindling in him.

The clerk frowned. "The only way for a man to stay healthy here is to state his business quick."

"I had a feeling I was riding through a no man's land," Sage said.

"You were feeling right, stranger. If you haven't got pretty urgent business in these parts, I'd advise you to keep moving."

Sage nodded silently, looking at some candy under the glass. This was the second warning he'd been given within the last hour. And he had no intention of heeding either of them. But this wasn't the time to say so.

"Maybe you're right, friend," he said. "I'll take a dozen of those peppermint sticks."

The clerk counted out the candy sticks. "Anything else?"

"Guess not. My sweet tooth is all that's aching." Sage dropped a quarter on the counter and, while he waited for his change, looked over the other customers.

They were ranching people, and there was a woman in the group whom he hadn't noticed before. She was young, but her open-throated shirt and denim pants placed her in the same class as the cowmen around her. She was tall, almost as tall as some of the men, and her battered hat was pushed far back off her blonde hair.

Sage turned back to the counter to pick up his change. "By the way," he said, "I heard talk about changing the name of this town. Anything to it?"

He saw instantly that he had touched a sore spot. The clerk's face pulled down in a scowl, and he shot a glance at the others along the far counter.

"That's a lie," he said heavily. "This town is Stirrup and it's going to stay that."

The girl came halfway across the room to Sage. "What other name was suggested, cowboy?"

Sage turned to face her, noticing the husky tone of her voice. "Someone said it would soon be called Eden," he said.

"Forget it," the girl said. "There'll be gun talk in this valley before Ferris changes the name of the town, too."

"You said it, Tess," the clerk agreed. "We let Ferris change the name of the creek to Eden Creek, and he calls the valley Eden Valley, but if he changes the name of this town, he'll do it over my dead body."

Sage picked up his sack of candy. "Looks like Ferris is an explosive subject," he said softly, and went out the door.

He walked to his horse and dropped the sack of

candy in the saddle bag. Time now to meet the other segment of Stirrup society. He started across the street, then stopped as a man and a young woman came out of the grocery.

These were homesteaders. Theirs was the road cart, and they climbed in and turned the horse away from the hitchrack. Even at that distance Sage could see that the girl was young and not hard to look at.

Then suddenly he went tight inside as he saw one of the shafts break loose from the harness and spring into the air, tipping the cart backward. The added strain on the other shaft broke the leather holding it, and it, too, shot up, tipping the cart backward.

The man was thrown into the street, but the girl clung to the low sides of the cart. The horse, startled, began to run. Sage didn't have time to think what he should do. The horse was coming down the street toward him, and the girl was still hanging to the cart.

He leaped into the street, waving a hand to slow down the horse. The horse was frightened but not yet crazy with fear. He veered away from Sage, and the cowboy grabbed at the bridle, caught it and pulled the animal down before it had hit its full stride.

"Anybody hurt?" he called, snubbing the snorting horse.

"I'm not," the girl said, swinging her feet around and over the back of the cart seat. "I don't know about Daddy."

She ran back up the street. Sage quieted her horse a little, then led him back, the cart dragging behind, shafts pointed toward the sky. The man was on his feet, brushing the dust from his clothes, apparently unhurt.

"I want to thank you, young man," he said politely, "for your heroic act. No doubt you saved my daughter from serious injury and unquestionably you kept our cart from being destroyed. We would find it very difficult to replace the cart."

Sage nodded but said nothing for a moment. This was an odd man to find in Stirrup. Obviously a very well educated man, he spoke in a soft, yet forceful voice, and his words had the deep ring of sincerity in them. His clothes were worn and patched, yet clean and neat. He carefully flipped the last of the dust off his narrow-brimmed hat and set it precisely on his head. He came only to Sage's shoulder when he stood erect and he was at least thirty pounds lighter. His blue eyes held the innocence of a babe when he looked at Sage.

But Sage found his attention shifting to the man's daughter. In Sage's estimation, she was about the prettiest girl he had ever seen; short, and with jet black hair that had slipped loose from some of its pins. Her eyes matched her hair. Also, there was a soft friendliness in her eyes and face that held his attention more than any one feature.

"I can't imagine what caused those straps to break," the girl said after a silence.

Sage turned to look at the harness. One glance was all he needed. "Somebody with a sharp knife helped," he said. "Cut both straps almost in two. Your weight broke one and the sudden jerk broke the other."

The girl's black eyes lost some of their friendliness. "I can guess who did that."

"Easy, Debbie," the man said gently. "We mustn't judge people."

Sage frowned. What manner of man was this? As if in response to his silent question, the man spoke to him.

"My name is John Ferris," he said, holding out his hand. "And this is my daughter, Deborah."

Sage shook Ferris' hand and was surprised at the man's firm grip. "I'm Jim Sage," he said.

"I'll get some wire and fix the harness. When I get home," Ferris said, "then I can do the job right. I'd like to pay you for your help, Mr. Sage, but all I can offer is my hospitality. You're welcome at our place any time. It's south and a little west of here."

Sage grinned. "I just might accept that invitation. I'm footloose right now, and a good home-cooked meal would be the best pay in the world."

He looked straight at the girl, and a smile tugged at her lips before she dropped her eyes. Then he looked at John Ferris again. This was the man the cattlemen were cursing. How could such a peaceable, soft-spoken man be the power that was threatening the cattle kings? It puzzled Sage.

He helped Ferris wire the leather loops back to the harness and watched the man and his daughter leave town. The girl, Debbie, lifted a hand in a brief wave.

Sage turned toward the grocery store from which they had come. There were only two customers and the clerk in sight. One of these customers caught his attention almost immediately. He was short and heavy-set, with a face that reminded Sage of a bulldog. Close-set beady eyes glared at him as he came in from the street. Like Ferris, he wore old patched overalls, but there was nothing clean or neat about the man.

"Something you want?" the clerk demanded, and there was open hostility in his voice.

"Just passing the time of day," Sage said easily.

"Pass it quick," the clerk said. "If you're just loafing, your store is on the other side of the street."

"Didn't know I had a store," Sage said softly.

"You're a cowman," the man snarled.

"This is the first place I ever found where that seemed to be a crime," Sage said. "But you've got the wrong bull by the horns. I'm not a cattleman; only a man who likes a saddle better than a plow."

"Either way, you're off your range here," the man snapped. "Who are you?"

"The name is Jim Sage. Now you might return the compliment."

"I'm Nate Munn, if that means anything to you."

Sage shrugged. "It doesn't. You look like you belong in the same corral with Ferris. But you act like you ought to be locked up in a bullpen."

"Listen, cowboy." Munn strode up to within a foot of Sage. "We saw you stop Ferris' horse and make up to them. Anybody can pull the wool over John Ferris' eyes. But you ain't fooling us none. You belong with the ranchers, and we don't want no part of you."

"Thanks for making it plain, Munn. The feeling is mutual. But I've got a bad habit of going where I feel like going. It will take more than you to stop me."

Red poured up into the snarling face of the homesteader. He pushed forward until his nose was right at Sage's chin. "I've stopped a lot of men bigger than you, cowboy. And I reckon I can stop you."

"Want to try it?" Sage challenged.

"Not in here," the clerk yelled. "If you're going to bust him, Nate, do it outside."

"You heard him," Munn growled, jerking his head toward the door. "Outside."

"Right after you,' Sage said tightly, following Munn to the door.

Munn went through the door, then turned suddenly as Sage was stepping over the sill and drove a fist into Sage's face. Sage had no chance to duck, and Munn's charge pushed him back. But he caught the casing of the door with his elbows and balanced himself. Then he lowered his head and drove away from the wall, pushing the shorter man out onto the porch.

Suddenly he stopped, snapping two hard punches to Munn's face. Munn reeled back against a porch post, blood spurting from his mashed nose. But he was far from whipped. Sage had seen his kind before and knew he had a battle on his hands.

Munn closed in, swinging his fists hard. The blows carried the kick of a mule, but they were too slow to catch a wary fighter like Sage. Sage gave ground, timing his moves carefully, stepping in to land stinging punches, then dodging out of reach of Munn's wild swings.

Munn's forward progress slowed as two new cuts on his face started to ooze blood. He made a last desperate effort to break through Sage's guard and hammer him down. And Sage chose that moment to move inside the man's wild punches and drive home two hard blows to the face. Munn back-peddled to the edge of the porch, lost his balance, and sprawled on his back in the dust under the hitchrack.

Sage leaned a hand against a post. "Get up, Munn," he said in disgust. "You'll spook the horses."

Munn got to his feet, spitting blood. "You'll see the day you'll regret this," he said thickly.

"Save your breath," Sage snapped. "Next time you won't get off so easy."

Sage turned across the street toward his horse, ignoring the muttered curses of Munn as he went back into the store.

Sage flipped the rein of his horse loose from the hitchrail. It was time to shake the dust of the town for a while. The pot was too near the boiling point for him to skim much information off the top.

He was just swinging into the saddle when a voice

from the porch hailed him. "Get banged up much, cowboy?"

Sage settled himself in the saddle and looked at the girl the clerk had called Tess. She was standing on the edge of the porch, arms folded, a speculative smile on her lips.

"I think I'll live through it," he said, waiting for her next move. She hadn't come out here to talk about his bruises.

"Looking for a job?" she asked finally.

"I haven't been exactly straining my eyes," he said slowly. "But that isn't saying I wouldn't consider one if everything suited me."

Her eyes strayed to the gun in the holster low on his right thigh. "I think this one will suit you. What's your name?"

"Sage. Jim Sage."

She nodded. "I'm Tess Brantley. I own the TS spread just west of town. Go on to the ranch and toss your gear in the bunkhouse. Then come up to the house tonight."

II

A light brightened a window in the TS ranch house, and Sage headed that way. At his light knock, Tess Brantley opened the door. She had discarded the working clothes she had been wearing in town in favor of a slim-waisted dress trimmed with ruffles. Her hair was in a neat bun on her head, and she had adorned it with a flower evidently picked from the flower bed Sage had noticed in front of the house.

"I hardly knew you," he said, realizing he had been staring.

She laughed. "Thanks for the compliment."

He seated himself in a chair by the table. "Do you always fix up like this to talk business?"

She laughed softly. "No. You saw my business outfit today."

"I thought I was invited here tonight for business."

She seated herself across from Sage. "Sometimes

business and pleasure mix, regardless of what they say."

He nodded slowly. "Could be."

"Well, business first." The teasing smile left her face and her eyes grow speculative as she looked at Sage. "I picked you for a man who wears his gun for a purpose. Am I right?"

His guard came up. He was matching wits with a clever woman.

"I can use my gun if necessary."

"Would a hundred a month make it necessary?"

He slowly shook his head. "A hundred dollars is pretty small when it's a man you're shooting at. But if the cards were right, I might work for less than a hundred."

She smiled. "I thought you'd say something like that. Principle outtalks money with you."

"Anything wrong with that?"

"It's a good failing." She tapped a finger on the table. "I think you'll like the job I have for you. I presume you're not overly fond of sodbusters. I saw your fight with Munn."

"Munn is a quarrelsome fellow."

"He's a sodbuster," Tess said. "If you saw things their way, you wouldn't have fought with him."

"You're looking for a gunslinger to put fear into the homesteaders?"

"Not exactly," she said slowly. "There's a good chance that you'll be earning big money for doing nothing."

Sage waited for her to elaborate, but she only drummed her fingers on the table, watching him from half-closed eyes.

"I bet my chips once before I found out it was a stacked deck," he said slowly. "Once was enough."

"What do you want to know?"

"You know that better than I do. Who are these homesteaders and why are they perched out there on that dried-out prairie? And what is this I hear about a dam on the creek?"

She sighed. "You've heard a lot. And I can tell you a lot more. When you see what your job is to be, I think you'll jump at it. A man named Ross Hampton owned the Flying H just west of this place. He was supposed to be a cattleman, but he got a crazy notion to build a dam up there and irrigate all this flat south of the creek. He sold a bunch of sodbusters on the idea, and they moved in, lock, stock, and barrel."

"I didn't see any irrigation ditches."

"There aren't any and there aren't going to be any.

That flat land is the best grazing in the country. Do you think the ranchers around here are going to let those clodhoppers turn that grass under?"

"But the settlers are already there. You said so."

Tess nodded. "They're there, all right. But they can't stay if they don't get water. And we're going to see that they don't get water. The dam is started, but it will never be finished."

Sage nodded, beginning to understand. "You want me to take the job of seeing that the dam isn't finished?"

Tess smiled. "You're getting close. You're a cow-man. You look it and act it. You don't want to see that flat land plowed under."

"You've got me pretty well tagged," he said slowly. "But what can I do to stop Hampton's dam?"

"Hampton isn't there any more," Tess said. "He met with an accident.'

Sage frowned a little. "What kind of an accident?'

"Got tangled in a rope and was dragged to death. I've never heard the details. But it stopped work on the dam."

"Then what is there for me to do?"

"Ross had been talking lately of a brother who was coming to help him. This brother, according to Ross, is a handy man with a gun and very likely can cause us a lot of trouble if he goes ahead with the dam."

"What's this brother's name?" Sage asked tightly.

"I don't know. I don't think Ross ever mentioned it. It was always 'my kid brother.' Your job will be to see to it that kid brother doesn't get to the Flying H and start work on that irrigation system."

The breath slid out of Sage.

"You think I can stop this brother?"

"I'm hiring you to try. That's all anybody can do. How about it?"

Sage hesitated. "I'd like to look over things here. Like I say, I got the deck stacked on me once. I don't aim to let it happen again."

"Sure," Tess said easily. "Look all you want to. There are about a dozen homesteader families out on the flats now. They'll be starved out by spring, I reckon, and move on unless the dam goes in and they're sure of irrigation."

"They'll fight for that flat, too, if there's a chance of their making a go of it," Sage added.

She nodded. "More than likely. But they aren't going to get that chance. If they should make a scrap, I think we can hold them off."

"We? Who else?"

"There are two or three more ranches below town that will be affected by this dam. We need the water as well as the grass."

"What about your water rights?"

"Hampton had first rights. He got here first and had foresight enough to land those rights. We're out of luck legally. But as long as he doesn't dam up that water, we'll get all we want."

"Who will be your biggest help if it comes to shooting trouble?"

"Clem Yake. He runs the Circle Y iron just below town. Big outfit. Has a dozen riders."

Sage nodded and got to his feet. "How about holding that job open for me?" he said. "I don't like sodbusters any better than most saddle men. But I want to look over the whole layout. While I'm looking, I'll keep an eye open for young Hampton."

Tess followed him to the door. "Fair enough, Jim. You'll be free to come and go on the TS as you please. Clem and I have talked it over. We're not particular how Hampton is stopped from working on that dam. But he's got to be stopped. It's our finish if he isn't."

Sage nodded. "I understand. You'll be hearing from me."

III

Sage left the TS the next morning without seeing Tess.

A mile south of the TS buildings, he reached the edge of the hills that formed the southern border of the valley, avoiding the homesteads which were mostly to the east. Over the first rim of hills, Sage swung his horse to the west and circled back toward the bluff that he had seen yesterday crowding in on the creek. He came out on the bluff above the creek and reined up.

Upstream a dike had been raised along one side to protect a gully that ran back into the bluff. Directly below him the grass had been scraped away and stakes set out, marking the course of the proposed irrigation ditch.

Sage knew little about irrigation but this set-up

looked like a good one. The flat plain south of the creek stretched away below the dam. There would be plenty of storage space for the water behind the dam. The creek was spring fed, he had heard, which meant it wouldn't dry up through the hot part of the summer. Proof of that was the steady stream of water running down there now.

He switched his eyes upstream, looking for Ross' headquarters, and saw the house and barn back to the south of the creek. They were up on a slope where the backwater from the dam would not touch them. The little meadow below the house would be inundated if the dam was completed.

Reining his horse toward the buildings, Sage dropped ofl the bluff and crossed the little meadow. He saw a man at the little corral behind the barn watching his approach. As he drew near, his eyes ran over the buildings. They were small, no bigger than the ones on the TS, and they were in poor repair. He had supposed that Ross' spread was a big, prosperous one. Evidently he had been wrong.

He cut away from the trail and reined over to the man, who had not moved. He was a tall slim man with a freckled face and flaming red hair that poked out from under his hat. His bright blue eyes were staring steadily at Sage.

"Howdy," Sage said amiably, and started to dismount.

The man held up his hand. "Better state your business, stranger, before you get down. You may not be staying long."

Sage dropped back in the saddle, frowning. "You're a friendly jasper, aren't you?"

"Maybe I am; maybe I ain't," the redhead said. "It's all according to who you are and what you want."

For the last hour Sage had debated with himself whether or not to reveal his real identity.

"You're Red Hoyt, foreman here, aren't you?"

The redhead nodded. "That still doesn't state your business."

Sage hesitated another minute, studying the face under the red hair. He liked what he saw and decided to take a chance. "I'm Sage Hampton. Mean anything?"

For a minute Hoyt stared at Sage; then he grinned and heaved a sigh. "It means plenty. Get down." He stepped forward as Sage dismounted and held out his hand. "Sorry I showed my horns. But things ain't been going right around here."

Sage nodded. "So I understand. I rode in yesterday."

"Where did you stay last night?"

"At the TS."

Suspicion flashed over Hoyt's freckled face. "That don't make sense."

Sage grinned. "Tess Brantley thought she was keeping a man named Jim Sage. I was offered a job making sure Ross Hampton's kid brother didn't come up and start work on that dam."

A grin broke over Hoyt's face. "That's a rich one. I'd sure like to see Tess when she finds out who you really are." His face sobered. "But it won't be healthy for you then."

"I haven't taken the job yet," Sage said. "But she's holding it open for me. I told her I wanted to look around a bit before I decided."

"Come on up to the house," Hoyt invited. "Reckon you'll want to hear what I know about all this. I should have recognized you the minute I saw you from the description Ross gave me. Never heard him tell anybody much else about you except that you were mighty handy with a gun."

Sage led his horse to the hitchrack in front of the house and followed Hoyt inside. "Anybody else working here?"

"Just two riders. They're out checking on the cattle we've got. They're running back in the hills. Ain't many. Ross did have a half-dozen men with teams working for him building the dam. You probably saw the dam when you rode in."

Sage nodded. "Do you think that's a good idea? Irrigating that flat so the nesters will plow up the grass, I mean."

The talkative redhead nodded vigorously. "I sure do. This country is mighty dry, but that ain't going to keep the sodbusters from swarming in here and tearing up that grass. Might as well water it and make it yield something beside dust storms. There's a lot more money for the Flying H in selling water than there is in cattle."

"You see things Ross' way, then?"

"Exactly. A couple of the boys here on the Flying H didn't, and Ross gave them their time. He was sold on the idea. But it stirred up a hornet's nest among the ranchers. It cost Ross his life."

"You think the ranchers killed him?"

Hoyt's face was grim. "Who else would do it? They had a good reason for wanting him stopped. The nesters had every reason to help him get the dam built. It was the nesters that he had hired."

Sage nodded. "Just what happened, Red? I've got to know, because that is my first job here—to find out who killed Ross and square accounts."

"I figured you'd be like that from what Ross said about you." Hoyt paused while he lit a cigarette he had rolled. "Ross had run-ins with every rancher down the creek after he announced his plans to build a dam. First they tried to stop him in court, but that didn't get them anywhere. Ross had the water rights tied up. They tried several tricks to delay work, but we got along pretty fast anyway."

Hoyt went to the window and stared out on the meadow. "Ross had a half-dozen arguments with Tess Brantley, too. But they never got too hot. Ross and Tess were friendly but on opposite sides of the fence."

"Pretty high fence, it seems," Sage put in. "She hinted pretty broad that she wasn't particular how the dam was stopped or what happened to Ross' kid brother."

Hoyt nodded. "She'll try to get her own way, all right. But I figure she's square."

"You say Ross had trouble with some other ranchers?"

"All of them. But Clem Yake was the main one. He's the one who will lose the most if we get the dam finished. He's got a big spread, and he uses most of that flat land for his winter range. Besides, he's got the silly notion that there won't be any water in the creek to water his cattle if we shut it off up here."

"Will there?"

"Sure. There are springs all the way along the bank of the creek. If we'd stop every drop of water here, which we won't, there would be a little stream running by the time it got to the TS, and plenty down at the Circle Y. Ross tried to tell him that, but he was so bull-headed he wouldn't listen."

"Do you think Yake might have killed Ross?"

Hoyt shrugged. "If you want my personal opinion, I'd say yes. Ross and Yake got into a row in Stirrup one afternoon last week. It was a mighty pretty fight, and Ross licked the daylights out of Yake. I figure that gave him the push he needed to murder Ross. But there is no proof."

"How did it happen?"

"Five days ago," Hoyt said, "Ross went to town in the afternoon. He said he'd be back late, so we didn't think anything about it when he didn't show up for supper. But by ten o'clock we got worried. So we struck out to find him. We couldn't find him in town or anywhere along the trail; not even his horse. We got back here about three in the morning, I guess, and found him by the corral. A piece of rope was still looped around him. It was a sickening sight."

"He'd been dragged to death?"

"That's what it looked like. We didn't move him. I rode back to town and got Doc Merrick. He's the coroner, too. Doc got here by sunup and took the body in. He pronounced it death by dragging."

"It would take a cowman to rope a man off a horse."

Hoyt nodded thoughtfully. "That's right. But here's something else to chew on. Anybody could tie a rope on a man that was already down."

"What do you mean by that?" Sage demanded quickly.

"I wouldn't bet my saddle that Doc hit it when he said death by dragging."

"You said there was a rope on him when you found him."

"There was," Hoyt admitted, tossing away his cigarette and rolling another one. "It was cut. Ever see a cowboy cut a rope instead of flipping it loose?"

Sage nodded. "I see what you mean. Somebody wanted us to think he'd been roped and dragged."

"Could be," Hoyt said, gazing out the window. "That rope wasn't frayed much, either, like it would have been if it had been dragged far over the sage-brush."

"Who would that point to, then?"

Hoyt shook his head and sighed as he turned away from the window. "It don't point to anybody, I guess. Just something I thought I'd pass on to you."

"But you seemed convinced that Clem Yake was guilty."

"I haven't changed my mind. He's the one who had every reason to want to kill Ross. But cutting that rope just doesn't sound like Yake."

"Reckon I'd ought to talk to Yake," Sage said slowly.

"Good idea. But don't wear gloves. He's hot-headed, and he packs an iron all the time."

"I stopped wearing gloves years ago," Sage said softly. "It doesn't look like I'll be starting here."

"Rid easy and sleep light," Hoyt advised. "Will you be making this your headquarters?"

"Not for a while. Remember, I've got a job on the TS as Jim Sage. I wouldn't want to run out on that, at least not till I've pumped the well of information dry. No telling what I might pick up."

"A dose of hot lead if you're not careful," Hoyt said. "You're playing with fire."

"I'll try not to get singed. Jim Sage can find out more in a day than Sage Hampton could in a month. He'll be safer, too."

"I reckon. I guess I've told you all I know. Any time you need help, you know where to get it."

Sage went back into the yard. "If I get up a dry wash, I'll whistle."

He left the Flying H, going back over the trail that led by the proposed dam. Once past Tess Brantley's ranch, he urged his horse to a faster pace. He wanted to see Dock Merrick, and pronto.

The town showed even less activity than it had yesterday. He found the office he was looking for tucked in between a drugstore and the barbershop. Only a flat sign above the door proclaimed its presence.

Sage went inside, dropped in a chair and relaxed in the coolness. A door into the back of the building opened and a small, graying man came out. He wore high-heeled boots and tight fitting pants. Sage might have taken him for a cowboy in town for Saturday except for the professional gaze he gave his visitor.

"You Doc Merrick?" Sage asked, getting to his feet.

The man nodded. "I am. What can I do for you?"

"Plenty, I reckon. I want to ask some questions."

Merrick nodded again, his eyes scrutinizing Sage. "Go ahead. I'll tell you whether I'll answer or not."

"You're the coroner, I hear."

"That's right."

"What do you know about Ross Hampton's death?"

Merrick turned and went slowly back to a little desk in the corner. "Why are you interested?"

"He was a friend of mine. I'm Jim Sage. I came out here to see Ross. I heard you had the last look."

"I did. The verdict was death caused by dragging."

"I'm not interested in verdicts," Sage said. "I want to know what you found out."

A frown tugged at Merrick's face. "I made out that verdict."

"That's all right," Sage said evenly. "That looks good in the records. Now I want to know what you really found out."

"I told you," the doctor said irritably. "Death by dragging."

"I heard you the first time," Sage said, leaning forward to stare at the doctor. "But it seems mighty funny a man could be dragged to death and the rope around him wouldn't be raveled out. And it isn't natural for a man who would rope another man and drag him to death to cut his rope rather than flip it loose."

The doctor lit a cigarette, took one puff and crushed it in a little bowl on his desk. "Who have you been talking to?"

"Somebody who was there ahead of you, Doc."

"Red Hoyt?"

Sage nodded. "Anything wrong with Hoyt?"

"Nothing except he's too nosy."

"Ross wasn't killed by dragging, was he, Doc?"

The lines in Merrick's face deepened, then hardened as determination came into his eyes. "No, he wasn't. He was beaten to death with a heavy club. It wasn't evident at first. Those gashes on his head could have come from dragging. But I saw what Hoyt saw and looked closer."

"Then why did you give the verdict you did?"

"This valley is ready to explode in our faces as it is. Everybody has been told that Ross Hampton met with an accident. Apparently most people believe it. We didn't tell how he was dragged to death. If the truth were known, I'd soon be the busiest man in the state."

"There are men here, then, who would try to avenge Ross' murder?"

Merrick nodded, lighting another cigarette and puffing nervously on it. "If they knew it was murder, half of those homesteaders out south of town would arm themselves with everything from rifles to butcher knives and head for the ranchers who have been fighting this irrigation ditch Hampton was trying to put in."

"Don't you have any law?"

"Sure. Down at Cottonwood. But that isn't doing us any good here. Before the sheriff could solve the crime, we'd have a dozen more murders. Better let it go this way."

"Have you any idea who did it, Doc?" Sage asked after a pause.

"No. And I'm not looking for ideas. You'd better do the same. Even if Hampton was a friend of yours, walk easy. I like the job of doctor better than being coroner."

"You think it was a planned murder, do you?"

"I didn't say that," Merrick said quickly. "I wish Hoyt had kept his mouth shut. If you've got any sense, you'll let well enough alone."

Sage leaned forward. "If your best friend was murdered, would you forget it?"

The doctor's lips were thin lines. "There are a hundred people who may suffer if you stir up this thing. You can't do your friend Hampton any good by getting a dozen more men killed."

"I won't be poking any fires. But I'm going to find out a few things. Thanks for your help, Doc."

"Don't you spread around what I told you."

Sage turned in the doorway. "So far as I'm concerned, I haven't even seen you."

IV

The road swung to the west, and Sage saw a house, built entirely above ground, just to the north of the road. That house, standing taller than the dugouts he had seen, must belong to John Ferris.

He reined up at a short hitchrack standing thirty feet from the south door. Along the front of the house was a small flower garden and beyond the house was a vegetable garden, the corner of which Sage could see now.

Sage dismounted and tied his horse, then started up the path between rows of zinias, marigolds, and other flowers he couldn't name.

John Ferris opened the door just before Sage reached it. "Come in, friend," Ferris said. "We're glad to see you."

Sage stepped inside, studying the little man who had

opened the door. "I was riding this way and thought I'd take advantage of your invitation," he said, looking around for Ferris' daughter.

"It's mighty hot," Ferris said, seating himself and motioning to another chair that was bettered and beaten but still held the dignity of a once fine piece of furniture. "It's the kind of weather to test a man's faith."

Sage shook his head. "It doesn't look like farming country."

"It can be made into good farm land with water," Ferris said earnestly. "The Lord put it here for us to use, and if we don't use it, it will be our own fault."

Debbie, coming in from the other room of the two-room house, tried to rescue Sage.

"I don't imagine Mr. Sage came here to be preached to, Daddy," she said as she crossed the room to her father.

"I wasn't preaching, Debbie," Ferris said gently. "I was just expressing my views. It wasn't meant for us to get something for nothing. The Lord helps those who help themselves, you know."

Debbie smiled understandingly at her father. "We're not being very neighborly, Daddy. We're talking, and I doubt if Mr. Sage has had his dinner."

Ferris straightened quickly. "I'm sorry. Of course

he hasn't had dinner. In fact, we haven't had ours. You'll eat with us."

It was a flat assertion rather than a question. Sage was on the point of objecting. But he checked himself. It would be an insult to refuse their hospitality. And he didn't want to insult the Ferrises, especially Debbie.

He watched the girl as she turned to the dinner that had been warming on the stove. She stuffed buffalo chips into the little cook stove, and the fire roared. Then he turned to John Ferris, who had become silent, his head lowered in thought.

"Fuel may be a problem here this winter with so many settlers on such a small strip of land," he said.

Ferris roused himself and nodded. "It will be. We're used to trees and plenty of wood to burn, but we can get all the buffalo chips we need back in the hills to the south. Just a little more work to gather them."

Debbie set a plate of hot biscuits on the table. "You look like a rancher, Mr. Sage," she said. "You ride like one and you talk like one. Do you think like one, too?"

"I don't know exactly how a rancher is supposed to think," Sage said evasively. "I've spent my life in a saddle, it's true, but I'm not looking for homesteaders' scalps today."

"You shouldn't challenge his motives, Debbie," Ferris reproved her gently. "He is our guest."

Sage grinned. "I disagree with you, Mr. Ferris. If I were in her place, I'd challenge every saddle man who came near these homesteads. They won't all be stopping by to make friends."

After dinner, Debbie showed Sage her vegetable garden, and Sage was surprised at the size and quality of it. There was enough there to stock the Ferrises' cellar for the entire winter.

"Who carries the water for this garden?" he asked.

"I carry most of it," she said as though it were a routine matter. "Daddy helps some, but he can't stand much heavy work."

Sage switched the conversation to the neighbors, and Debbie talked freely. There were a dozen families in the little colony, the closest neighbor being Cal Ufford, a bachelor and a leader in church work with John Ferris back in Indiana whence they had come.

"Who lives in that first house south of the creek? It's off to the east of the road by itself."

"That's Abe Masterson," Debbie said. "He liked that plot of ground and said he'd dig his own ditches from ours down to him. He has a wife and one little girl."

"What would happen if you didn't get irrigation?"

Sage asked after they had moved around to the shade on the east side of the house.

"We'd be starved out," the girl said practically. "But the dam will be finished."

"Who's going to do it now that Ross Hampton is dead?"

Debbie sighed. "Ross had a brother he said would finish the job if anything happened to him. We're waiting for him to come."

Sage read the hope and the despair mingled in her voice. Their one hope of survival here was water, and that hope rested on Ross Hampton's brother. Sage felt like a traitor. Here he stood, the man they were waiting for. And he was a saddle man; a man who couldn't see turning under fine grazing land even when the virtues of it were explained to him by the prettiest girl he had encountered in many a moon.

"Here comes Cal," Debbie said suddenly.

Sage jerked up his head. A tall, loose-jointed man was striding up the road toward the Ferris homestead. He was thin and awkward-appearing, and as he got closer, Sage could see the long uncut sandy hair brushing out from under his narrow-brimmed hat. His pale blue eyes settled on Sage a minute before he got to the house, and they remained fixed on him even after he came to a halt ten feet from them.

"Hello, Cal," Debbie said with a smile. "This is Jim Sage, Calvin Ufford."

Sage took a step forward, but stopped when Ufford made no move to shake hands or acknowledge the introduction.

"What's he doing here, Debbie?" he said. And his voice, a deep bass, carried a rasping edge. "He belongs on the ranchers' side of the fence."

"He's here as a friend," Debbie said quickly. "He stopped our runaway in town yesterday."

"Probably using that as a wedge to work into our good graces."

Sage was finding it hard to give Ufford the respect he held for John Ferris. He looked sullen and quarrelsome and he wasn't showing any regard for Debbie's opinion.

"I'll admit I came out today because they invited me to stop by sometime," Sage said. "But I'm not carrying a banner for the ranchers."

"You're a saddle man."

Sage nodded. "But that doesn't mean I'm taking any cards in this fracas."

"Where did you come from?"

Sage saw Debbie frown at the question. But Sage

couldn't object. He had defended Debbie earlier when John Ferris had criticized her for similar questions.

"I came from a long way off and I expect to be going the same place some of these days," he said.

Ufford wasn't satisfied, but he seemed at a loss to find a more pointed question with which to pin Sage down.

"If he is a saddle man, Cal," Debbie said, crossing to the tall farmer, "then he's a stranger in a strange land. Are we treating him as we should?"

Ufford bit his lip and looked at the ground. "I guess not, Debbie. Sorry, fellow, but we have reasons to be jumpy and suspicious."

Sage nodded. "I've been getting that impression everywhere I turn. John Ferris is the only one who didn't seem to think so."

Ufford frowned. "He is too trusting."

"But everybody trusts him, don't they?"

"Of course. Everybody knows John's word is better than most men's bond. Why wouldn't they trust him?"

"Then his trust isn't wasted," Debbie said quickly.

Sage thought he began to see why John Ferris held such a powerful position among the homesteaders. It wasn't every man who could command such trust. But trust and power didn't always go hand in hand.

Ufford turned and walked toward the house. "Is John awake?"

"He should be," Debbie said, following him.

Sage watched the tall man move around the corner of the house. Something about his walk was familiar. Where had he seen it before?

Debbie turned at the corner of the house. "Won't you come in, Mr. Sage?"

Sage shook his head. "I think it's time I was riding. Thanks for the meal."

Debbie smiled. "You're welcome. And come again."

"I reckon I'll do that."

Sage grinned and lifted a hand as he turned toward the barn to get his horse.

V

Sage unsaddled his horse at the TS corral and fed him. As he started toward the bunkhouse, the door of the big house opened and Tess Brantley came across the yard to intercept him.

"Find out a lot of things today, Jim?" she asked as he stopped.

Sage grinned as he waited for her to come up to him. She was wearing a shirt and Levis, but there was nothing masculine about the outfit or about her. She had left her hat in the house, and the late afternoon sun struck sparks from her honey-colored hair.

"I learned quite a few things," he said.

"Still want the job I offered you?"

"I'm still making this my headquarters."

"But you're not sure?" she pressed.

"I've been out looking over the homesteads," Sage

said slowly, wondering just how frank he should be with Tess Brantley. "I feel sorry for those squatters, but I don't like to see that good grass plowed under any better than you do."

Tess noddd. "I know what you mean. I have nothing against the nesters themselves except when they steal my beef and plow up my grass. That isn't good farm ground and never will be."

Sage didn't feel like arguing with her. She sounded more tolerant now than she had last night.

"I'll have supper ready in half an hour. I'll see you then."

"Don't I eat with the rest of the crew?" Sage asked as she turned away.

Tess stopped and looked back at him, a teasing smile on her lips. "Must I draw a picture to explain to you you're a special member of my crew?"

He grinned. "I'll be there in half an hour. And I'm warning you. I'm hungry."

"I'll see to it you get all you want," she said as she hurried toward the house.

But any ideas Sage might have had about a quiet secluded meal with Tess Brantley were shattered when a rider came out of the dusk and reined up at the house just as Sage was checking in for supper.

"That's Clem Yake," Tess said, setting a skillet of steak on the back of the stove and going to the door.

Sage's interest quickened. He had been wanting to get a look at the biggest rancher along Eden Creek. But the minute he stepped into the light, he realized he had seen him before. It had been Clem Yake he had met yesterday on the way to Stirrup.

Tess brought Yake into the center of the room, and Sage saw the excitement and anger on the big rancher's face. Yake took off his hat and ran his gnarled hand over his bald head. Sage remembered that gesture on the trail yesterday.

"More trouble, Tess," Yake said. "We've got to get rid of those nesters or they'll steal us blind."

"What this time, Clem?" Tess's voice was calm, but the lines of her face had hardened and her eyes were as cold as ice.

"Two more butchered: a yearling of mine and a two-year-old of yours."

"Any idea who?"

Yake shook his head. "It was a nester. That's all I know. If I knew which one, I'd ride down there personally and string him up."

"I'd go with you," Tess said bitterly. "I think it's time we did something besides talk."

Yake nodded. "So do I. What have you got in mind?"

"I've just two riders. But you've got a dozen. That ought to be enough. Nesters usually aren't very good fighters."

Sage cleared his throat and moved out of the corner where he had been standing. Tess wheeled toward him.

"I forgot about you. Jim, this is Clem Yake, Jim Sage."

Sage shook hands with the rancher, noting the firm grip. But he also saw the flash of recognition in Yake's eyes.

"You forgot your crew numbers three now, Tess," Sage said.

"Is he working for you?" Yake asked.

"For us," Tess said. "He hasn't said for sure what he'll do, but I'm trying to hire him to make sure no more work is done on that dam."

"What makes you think he'll do it?" Yake demanded.

"I saw him give Nate Munn the beating of his life in town yesterday, and the way he carries a gun shows he knows what to do with it."

"Did he tell you he was a friend of Ross Hampton?"

Tess whirled on Sage. "Is that right?"

Sage nodded. "Ross Hampton was a good friend of mine."

"Why didn't you tell me?" Anger was rising in Tess.

"You didn't ask me," Sage said. "I didn't see how it affected what you wanted me to do."

"Why wouldn't it?" Yake asked. "If you were a friend of Hampton's, you'd want to see his work finished."

"Not necessarily," Sage said evenly. "I happen to be a saddle man, and I don't like to see good grass turned under."

Yake and Tess exchanged glances. "You knew what Hampton was trying to do?" Yake asked finally.

"I found out a lot about it today."

"And you want to see the dam stopped?" Tess asked cautiously.

"I told you I don't think much of homesteaders. And I don't like sodbusters who butcher other people's beef."

"Would you want to ride with us when we run them out?"

Sage hesitated. "I don't think that's quite the way to do it. I know there are some settlers down there who wouldn't do a thing like that. There are others who probably would. I say, find the man who is responsible and make an example of him."

Yake snorted. "Just how do you propose doing that? We've tried it for two months and haven't found a trace of anything."

"Send a man down there to search until he finds the meat," Sage said.

"He'd get shot," Tess said. "Then we'd be one man short. The nesters would expect us to fight and dig in. We'd better surprise them."

Sage looked at Yake, but the rancher apparently had nothing to add. That was further proof to Sage that Tess Brantley was the real power among the ranchers in Eden Valley. He wondered just how much Clem Yake knew about Ross Hampton's murder. He had intended to ask Yake some questions when he saw him, but this was hardly the time.

"I reckon you're right, Tess," Yake said after a long pause. "We don't have any men who want to commit suicide."

"It wouldn't be suicide," Sage said. "Most men, even homesteaders, aren't killers."

"That sounds like John Ferris' reasoning," Tess accused him.

"I saw Ferris today," Sage admitted. "But I can't say that I agree with his cockeyed views."

"If you're so sure hunting that butchered beef is such a safe job," Yake said, "why don't you do it?"

Sage looked from Yake to Tess. It wasn't a job he wanted. At this rate he'd soon have everybody after his hide. But he was convinced it was the right way to go about the rustling problem.

"That's all right with me," he said finally. He looked at Tess.

Tess nodded. "You start in the morning. And when you find the beef, bring in the nester that stole it and I'll personally settle with him."

He cut across the prairie south of the creek until he hit the road, then followed it past several half-dugouts until he came to Ferris' soddy. There he swung down and was met by Debbie at the door.

"I wasn't expecting to see you again so soon," she said. "But you're welcome."

He followed her inside. "I'm afraid I won't be when you find out what I'm after."

John Ferris got up from his chair. "I hope it's nothing serious."

"I'm afraid it is," Sage said. "I'm looking for some beef that was butchered yesterday. It belonged to Clem Yake and Tess Brantley."

Color flooded over Debbie's face. "Surely you don't

think you'll find it here."

"Of course not," Sage said quickly. "But I do expect to find it somewhere among the homesteaders. I wanted to talk it over with you folks before I started looking."

"You'd better get back on your own side of the creek," Debbie said sharply, and there was an anger in her voice Sage hadn't supposed she possessed.

"Easy, Debbie," Ferris said gently. " 'The tongue is a little member, but behold how great a matter a little fire kindleth.' "

Debbie bit her lip. "Sorry, Daddy. But he has no right to accuse us of stealing cattle."

"I'm not accusing you," Sage said hastily. "I'm just trying to find who did butcher those two beeves."

"What makes you think someone in our colony did it?" Ferris asked.

"It's the only reasonable thing to think," Sage said. "If ordinary rustlers were working, they wouldn't stop at two. And they wouldn't butcher the cattle; they'd run them off. Clem Yake found the carcasses."

"There's no man in our group who would steal," Ferris said positively.

"I hope not. But I'm afraid you're wrong."

"Who do you suspect?" Debbie asked.

"No one in particular," Sage said. "I don't know these settlers. If they have nothing to hide, they shouldn't object to my looking."

"They will, though."

Sage nodded. "I'm afraid so. That's why I came here first. I've been told you are the leader of these settlers, Ferris. I want to get your permission to look for that beef."

"Don't let him do it, Daddy," Debbie said quickly. "It will just mean trouble."

"I thought yesterday maybe you would be a true friend," Ferris said. "Why do you come to trouble us now?"

Sage had his answer ready. "I happened to be around when word was brought in last night about the two steers being butchered. The ranchers were all for coming down here armed to the teeth and running every settler out. I suggested finding the one who was guilty and punishing him and letting the rest of you alone. They agreed and gave me the chore of finding the thief."

Ferris nodded. "And if you had balked about taking the job, they'd have come in and driven us all out?"

"That's about it," Sage said.

"I'm sorry, Mr. Sage," Debbie said softly. "I didn't

understand all the circumstances."

"Just another lesson, Debbie," Ferris said. "Patience is a golden virtue. It always pays to get the facts before voicing an opinion. I'm sure, Mr. Sage, you are wrong in suspecting any member of our colony. However, in order to prove to the ranchers that we are innocent, I'll give my permission for you to examine every house here."

Sage breathed easier. "Thanks, Mr. Ferris. I hope I don't find anything, but if there is a thief in your outfit, I'm sure you would want him uncovered."

Ferris nodded. "You're right. We have no place for thieves. Debbie, you ride along with Mr. Sage and explain his mission so there will be no misunderstanding."

Debbie nodded and got her hat.

They completed a fruitless search of the main part of the colony and angled down the slope to the last house, the one belonging to Abe Masterson. Sage hadn't found any beef and he was feeling much better. That butchering might well have been done by someone who wanted to stir up trouble between the ranchers and nesters. Maybe Yake himself had done it. Sage thought of that for a moment and discarded it. Clem Yake was not that good an actor. And Sage was inclined to believe that, regardless of what else he might be, Yake was honest.

Abe Masterson was fixing some harness in front of his little sod barn when Sage and Debbie rode up. He put down the harness and came to the house to meet them. He was a medium-sized man with friendly blue eyes that welcomed Debbie and ran inquisitively over Sage.

"Abe," Debbie said, "this is Jim Sage. A couple of steers were butchered and the ranchers sent him down here to see if some of our farmers had done it. Daddy gave him permission to look through the houses for the meat."

"When did that happen?" Masterson asked.

"Yesterday," Sage said. "Or at least Yake found what was left of the carcasses yesterday afternoon."

"This is the last house," Debbie said. "Then he can go back and tell Clem Yake and Tess Brantley that it wasn't the homesteaders who butchered their beef."

Debbie was confident. But she hadn't seen what Sage had seen. He had taken an instant liking to Abe Masterson, but now, as he watched the farmer's startled face, he was sure he had found the beef.

"What do you expect to find by searching our houses?" Masterson asked Sage.

"I'm looking for freshly butchered beef. It isn't likely any homesteader would butcher his milk cow." Sage swung down. "It won't take a minute to look."

A woman had come quietly to the door. She was dark and, Sage thought, rather pretty. He guessed her to be about thirty, three or four years younger than Masterson. A little girl, about six, clung to the woman's apron. She had blonde hair and the brightest blue eyes Sage had seen in a long time.

Masterson moved around between Sage and the house. "You have no right to search my house," he said.

The woman tugged at Masterson's sleeve. "What's wrong, Abe?"

"He's looking for beef, Ruth," Masterson said. "Claims the ranchers had some stolen."

Sage saw the woman catch her breath, and Debbie swung off her horse and came around to stand beside her.

Sage didn't try to push past Masterson. "You've got it, haven't you, Masterson?"

Masterson drew a deep breath. "I've got some fresh beef, yes. But I didn't do any butchering."

"How did you get it then?"

"I made a deal. I'm to work for a fellow for three

days to pay for the chunk I've got."

"Who did you get it from?"

Masterson appeared about to answer, then clamped his mouth shut. Sage looked at Masterson's wife and his little girl. The woman was close to tears and the child was frightened, her big eyes fixed on Sage as though he were a goblin.

"You can save yourself and your wife and little girl a lot of trouble if you'll tell me where you got the beef," Sage pressed.

"I'd just be passing my trouble to somebody else," Masterson said.

"If you didn't steal it, it isn't your trouble," Sage argued.

Masterson looked around at his wife and daughter and Debbie, then back at Sage. "I've told you all I'm going to."

Sage sighed. "Better get your horse and come along with me," he said.

Ruth Masterson caught her husband's arm. "No, no," she cried. "Don't go, Abe. They'll hang you."

Debbie ran up to Sage. "You fiend! Abe Masterson didn't steal that beef."

"I believe that," Sage said. "But he knows who did. That's what I came down here to find out. I'll turn him loose when he tells me who the thief is."

"You'll be holding me a long time," Masterson said.

"You'll let them hang him," Debbie cried, her hands squeezed into fists.

"There'll be two of us dead if they do that," Sage promised. "Tess Brantley and Clem Yake are hard customers, but they're fair. They won't hang Masterson."

"I suppose you aim to keep me prisoner," Masterson said.

"That's up to you," Sage replied. "You know how you can get out of it."

"I told you I won't say any more." He turned to Debbie. "Will you keep an eye on Ruth and Ramona, Debbie?'

"Of course, Abe," Debbie said.

Masterson got his horse, making no effort to escape. Sage, mounted and ready to go, made one last effort to get the name of the thief.

"You could tell me who sold Abe the beef, Mrs. Masterson," he said. "If you do, I'll leave Abe here."

Sage thought for a moment she was going to give him the information. Then she looked at her husband and shook her head. "If Abe won't tell you, I won't, either."

Sage reined around, directing Masterson to ride ahead, and they cut across the prairie toward the TS.

VI

Debbie took little time covering the mile and a half home. Cal Ufford was in front of his barn as she rode past, but at the moment she didn't want to stop to talk, even to Cal. When she dismounted in front of her father's soddy, she saw Cal coming down the road in long strides.

"Was Mr. Sage satisfied no homesteader had anything to do with stealing those steers?" John Ferris asked as Debbie came in the house.

"He's satisfied, all right," Debbie said angrily. "He took Abe Masterson with him back to the TS."

John Ferris leaned forward in his chair. "Why did he do that?"

"Abe had some fresh beef and wouldn't tell where he got it."

"Abe Masterson is no thief," Ferris said positively.

"Of course he isn't," Debbie said hotly. "Even Jim Sage admitted that. But he took him along because Abe wouldn't tell where he got it."

Ferris nodded slowly. "Abe should have told."

"I admire Abe for his courage," Debbie said quickly. "He didn't let that bully push him around."

"Let's not be too hasty in our judgment," Ferris said.

Cal Ufford came in without the formality of knocking. He looked from John Ferris to Debbie.

"What was your big hurry just now?"

"I was mad," Debbie said.

Ufford's eyebrows raised. "What stirred you up?"

"Jim Sage."

Ufford flashed a glance at Ferris, then back at Debbie. "That saddle man, eh? Don't tell me he found the beef."

"He found some at Abe Masterson's. And you know Abe wouldn't steal."

Ufford frowned and moved closer to Debbie. "What did Abe say?"

"He wouldn't tell who sold the beef to him," Debbie said.

Ufford nodded. "Abe Masterson is a courageous man. What did Sage do about it?"

"He took him to the TS."

Ufford seemed lost in thought for a moment. "I wonder what he thought he'd gain by that."

"Evidently he thought Abe would tell him who the real thief was," Ferris said from his chair by the window.

"Abe won't talk," Ufford said positively. "And Tess Brantley won't allow any rough treatment. It will come out all right."

Debbie shook her head. "The ranchers seem determined to find the thief who butchered their beef. They'll be more certain than ever now that somebody down here did it."

"That's right." Ufford slammed a fist into his palm. "Maybe we ought to beat them to the punch. They wouldn't be looking for us to take the bull by the horns."

"Cal," Ferris said sharply, "have you forgotten your scriptural teachings? 'Love thy neighbor.' 'Let not the sun go down upon your wrath.' "

Ufford pinched his lips together and said nothing for a minute. When he spoke, the harsh edge was gone from his voice.

"Sorry, John. These are circumstances to try our patience. But it's hard to love our neighbors when our neighbors include such men as Jim Sage. He obviously was here yesterday to spy on us."

Ferris shook his head. "He was here yesterday at our invitation and he came in good faith. I hold no malice toward Mr. Sage. I'm sure everything can be worked out peaceably if we but try."

"I hope so," Ufford said. But there was still a frown on his face. "I hope Sage never shows his face down here again."

Ufford went outside and, through the window, Debbie saw him going back toward his own homestead.

"When are you and Cal going to be married?" Ferris asked. "Perhaps you could give him the encouragement and stamina he needs for the work ahead."

"We haven't set a definite date," Debbie said. "It will probably be either this fall or next spring. I would so like to get things settled before we plan a wedding."

John Ferris nodded wearily. "Yes, I know, Debbie. I don't mean to be rushing you. But it isn't good for you to spend all your time here with me when you could be starting a happy home of your own."

"Let's talk about it later, Daddy," Debbie said. "I told Ruth Masterson I'd come back and stay with her until Abe gets home."

"That was a good thing to do, Debbie," Ferris said. "Stay all night with her or bring her back here if Abe doesn't get home tonight."

Debbie found Ruth Masterson calmly sewing in the one big room of the Masterson soddy. Little Ramona was playing in the yard with a box she called her playhouse. But her play was listless and her big blue eyes followed Debbie solemnly as she went into the house.

"You didn't stay home very long," Ruth said.

Debbie found a chair and tried to appear as relaxed as Ruth. "There was nothing to do there but tell Daddy where I would be."

"Abe will be home before long," Ruth said matter-of-factly. "But I do appreciate your staying with me till he comes."

Debbie helped Ruth get dinner, and it was ready when Abe rode into the yard. Ruth didn't appear particularly surprised, although there was relief on her face. Debbie found it hard to curb her curiosity.

While they ate dinner, Abe told about his brief stay at the TS and Tess's intervention and also the warning she had given him to pass on to the one who had sold him the beef.

"You say Clem Yake was there?" Ruth asked. "How did he take it when Tess sent you home?"

"He was plenty riled," Abe said. "But it looks to me like Tess holds the whip hand up there."

"You'd better stay away from town, Abe," Ruth cautioned. "You might run into Yake when Tess wasn't around."

Abe nodded. "I'll have to be careful, all right. I'm no gunman, and Yake is. But I do intend to go to town tomorrow afternoon."

Debbie leaned forward. "What for?"

"I met Red Hoyt on my way home. He said Ross Hampton's lawyer got in town this morning and he's going to read Ross' will publicly tomorrow afternoon."

"Publicly," Ruth exclaimed. "Why?"

"It seems it was Ross' request. I intend to be there to hear it read."

"But won't it be dangerous?" Ruth argued.

Abe shook his head. "I don't think so. Everybody wants to hear that will read. I imagine most of the homesteaders will be there. I'll be safe enough with them."

Debbie thought a lot about Ross Hampton's will as she rode home.

Instead of riding directly home, she reined off toward the hills to the south. John Ferris wouldn't be expecting her early tonight, so there was no hurry. She headed for her favorite spot, a knoll from which she could see the entire valley spread out below her. It was there that she went when she had a problem to think out.

She stopped her horse on the knoll and dismounted. It was hot but she hardly noticed. Below she saw the cluster of soddies that was the little homestead colony, and out beyond that, the rolling bottom lands to the creek. And she could see the Circle Y buildings far down to her right. Even from that distance she could tell it was a big ranch. The buildings and the windbreak were gigantic. Stirrup was almost directly in front of her across the creek, and upstream a mile or so was the TS.

The sound of a horse behind her snapped her out of her reverie. She whirled to face Jim Sage, who had stopped just below the crest of the knoll.

"Maybe I'm intruding," he said.

"You won't find any cattle thieves up here," Debbie said cuttingly.

He came on to the top of the little hill and dismounted. "I haven't found any anywhere yet. Tess Brantley sent Masterson home."

Debbie nodded. "I know. What else could she do? Abe didn't steal any beef."

"The only crime he committed was withholding the name of the real thief."

"I admire him for his courage," Debbie said.

"Sometimes courage can be misplaced."

"Faith can be, too." She nodded toward the gun he wore. "Faith placed in that will yield nothing but trouble and sorrow."

His face creased in a lopsided grin. "Sometimes a lack of faith in a gun will yield six feet of sod in a man's face."

"There are worse things."

"Maybe so. But after you stop a bullet there ain't much chance to find out what they are."

"You don't believe in anything that you can't get your hands on, do you?"

"Is there anything else?"

"If there wasn't, it would be a mighty dull world."

He shrugged. "I don't know about that. I find things pretty exciting sometimes. And I don't live by that 'love thy neighbor' rule, either. Do you honestly believe in that?"

Debbie nodded, exasperation forcing the words from her lips. "Of course I do. If everybody practiced that, there would be no trouble."

"But when half practice it and half don't, somebody's going to wind up holding the short end of the stick."

"It won't be those who practice peace and friendship to one another."

"It would take a lot of preaching to convince some people of that."

"I guess it would in your case," she said, fighting to keep the anger out of her voice.

She mounted her horse and put him at a lope down toward the cluster of homesteads.

VII

Tess came across the yard before Sage was ready to leave the next morning. "Where are you heading this morning, Jim?"

"Thought I'd ride up and take a look at the place where that dam is supposed to be," he said easily.

"Better come into town this afternoon and hear Hampton's will read. You'll find out what provisions Ross made to get that dam finished."

"You think he made plans to have that crazy project finished?"

Tess nodded. "I'll bet he did. He was a thorough man. And he was on the outs with a lot of people. If that accident hadn't happened, something else might have. I'll wager he thought of that and appointed somebody to go ahead."

Sage nodded, thinking suddenly that he was the

logical one to inherit the job. "But the fellow that draws the job may shy away from it."

"If he does," Tess said, "that will make your job pretty easy. If he doesn't, you ought to be there to see who you're going to have to stop."

"I'll look over the setup on the Flying H," he said as he mounted. "And I'll be in town this afternoon if I can make it."

He left the yard and splashed across the little creek, heading his horse upstream toward the Flying H. He wasn't particularly interested in the dam; he had seen it before. But there were questions that had come to mind since he had seen Red Hoyt the other day that he wanted answered.

Hoyt was at the corral when Sage rode into the Flying H. He came over to the fence as Sage reined up and dismounted.

"How are you making out with Tess?" Hoyt asked, his freckled face spread wide in a grin.

"We're still able to stay on the same ranch. What do you know about those nesters down there?"

Hoyt lifted his hat and ran a hand through his fiery hair. "Not too much. Old John Ferris is the ramrod, although you'd never guess it."

"I know that," Sage said. "I've been down there.

Had dinner with the Ferrises a couple of days ago. Yake and Tess each had a beef butchered the other day. They figure the nesters did it."

Hoyt frowned. "Maybe," he said. "They're mighty hard up. Meat looks pretty good to them."

"Which one would do that?"

"That's a little hard to say. Any man with hungry kids might do it. And I wouldn't blame him a lot."

"But it's stealing. And Tess and Yake don't intend to put up with it. I went down to the homesteads yesterday and tried to find the fresh beef."

Interest brightened Hoyt's face. "What luck?"

"I found the beef, or some of it. But I didn't find the thief. I figured you'd know those homesteaders better than anybody else and you could tell me who is most likely to be the thief."

Hoyt shook his head. "I haven't been looking for thieves down there."

"How about murderers?"

Hoyt's face turned grim. "That's a different story. I don't have a thing new. But I intended to show you that cut rope the other day and forgot it."

Hoyt led the way across the yard to the house. From a little sack behind the door he brought out a short piece of rope.

"Take a look at that," he said. "That was the rope that was around Ross. You can see it isn't frayed out like it would have been if it had been dragged far over this sagebrush. And look at the end."

Sage was looking. It was cut clean, and to Sage that meant a big sharp knife and a strong man wielding it.

"That might be of some help," Sage said musingly.

"I was hoping it would be. But how?"

"I'll keep an eye open for a big knife. No pocket knife did that."

Hoyt nodded. "I reckon not. A strong man might do it with a hunting knife if the rope was tight."

"Who carries a knife around here?"

"Can't think of anybody," Hoyt said slowly. "I'm sure Yake doesn't."

"Most men who carry guns don't bother with knives," Sage observed. "This makes less sense all the time."

Hoyt put the rope back in the little sack. "Going in to hear the will read, I suppose."

"I'll be there," Sage said. "We might find out something from Ross' will that will throw some light on his murder."

Hoyt nodded. "Could be."

"See you in town," Sage said, and went back to his

horse.

Stirrup was crowded. Sage rode down the length of the street before finding a place to tie his horse.

He turned into the grocery where the ranchers were congregating. The clerk looked up as Sage entered, and a scowl creased his face as he moved over to meet him.

"What are you looking for?" he demanded.

"A place to wait out of the sun," Sage said easily. He glanced over the crowd and saw Tess Brantley leaning against the counter talking to Clem Yake and one of the Circle Y riders.

"You can find another place," the clerk said sourly.

"I could," Sage said, frowning. "But I don't aim to look."

"I'll save you the trouble of looking," the clerk said angrily. "I'll show you."

Sage didn't budge. Apparently the clerk was intent on showing everybody he was king pin in his own store.

"Get out," the clerk snapped.

"I take my orders from Tess Brantley," Sage said, and leaned against the wall.

The clerk jerked his head around to look at Tess, then back at Sage. Finally he whirled and went back behind his counter. Evidently Tess had the final word there, too.

Sage tapped the arm of a man close to him. "Where is Trenton going to put on his show?"

"At the hotel," the man said.

"What time?"

"About two, I hear. That Hampton must have been a queer one to call for a public reading of his will."

"I reckon," Sage said, and moved back outside.

He found the tiny lobby of the hotel already nearly full. There were no chairs left, but he found a spot along the wall close to the door and leaned against it.

Sage was surprised when he saw the man who finally came through the door exactly on the stroke of two. He was a little man, scarcely over five and a half feet tall, and Sage guessed he didn't weigh more than a hundred and fifty pounds. He had wavy brown hair, and his brown eyes flashed excitedly over the waiting crowd.

The little fellow climbed up on the desk at the back of the lobby and held up a hand. "Can you hear me out there?" he shouted.

Heads nodded out in the street, and Trenton smiled as he looked over the crowd. "Ross Hampton asked me to read his will publicly in the event of his death within three years from the time he made it."

The lawyer paused.

"This will was made only six weeks ago, so there is little chance that Ross would have changed his mind about anything he has set forth here. He wanted, above all other things, to avoid trouble."

"Cut the speech making," a Circle Y rider shouted from the doorway. "We came to town to hear the will."

Trenton smiled indulgently. "You shall hear it, my friend." He opened a large envelope he carried and carefully unfolded a long legal-looking paper.

Trenton cleared his throat and stretched his neck as though to get more volume from his voice. "I, Ross Hampton, being of sound mind, do hereby leave all my earthly possessions, including the Flying H Ranch and other assets, to my brother, Sage Hampton, providing he meets the following requirements.

"The first provision," Trenton read loudly, "is that my brother must come to the Flying H and, providing it is not completed, complete the dam across Eden Creek and have the water running to the homesteads on Eden's Plain by October first of the year this is read."

A murmur swept through the crowd.

Trenton held up a hand for silence, and the voices ceased. "In the event the dam is completed, my brother must operate the irrigation project for at least one year.

If he fails to fulfill the provisions of this will, I then decree that my lawyer, Benjamin Trenton, shall open a sealed envelope which I have given him and follow the instructions he shall find there."

Trenton held up his hand again for silence. "Ross Hampton died before he completed the dam across Eden Creek, so the first provision of this will will go into effect. Ross' brother, Sage Hampton, must come to the Flying H and complete the dam and have water running to the homesteads by October first or he loses the ranch."

"What happens then?" Tess Brantley demanded.

Trenton reached into his pocket and drew out a long envelope. "Then I will open this envelope and follow the instructions in it."

"What are those instructions?"

Silence fell over the crowd. "I don't know what the instructions are," Trenton said. "Ross gave me this envelope sealed as you see it now. It is to be opened only in the event his brother fails to fulfill the provisions set forth in this will."

Cal Ufford pushed his way into the doorway and asked a question. "If Hampton's brother doesn't come and finish that dam, where will that leave us?"

Trenton turned sharp eyes on Ufford. "High and

dry, I imagine, my friend. At least dry."

A chuckle ran over the ranching section of the crowd. But Sage was watching the homesteaders. Ufford's face was impassive, showing nothing. But it was different with the others. Debbie Ferris was biting her underlip, and he was sure there was a trace of moisture in her eyes. John Ferris was trying hard to keep from showing how hard he had been jolted by the blow that had been dealt his dream. Abe Masterson was standing stony-faced against the railing of the veranda, but there was no mistaking the tears in Ruth's eyes.

"Well, that takes care of the nesters," the puncher next to Sage said.

"Not if the dam is finished by the first of October," Sage reminded him.

The puncher laughed. "Who's going to finish it? Nobody knows where this brother of Ross Hampton's is. And it's a cinch nobody else will put it in."

"Maybe Ross left the ranch to John Ferris in case his brother didn't claim it," Sage said, voicing a thought that had been nagging him.

The cowboy laughed again. "Not a chance of that. Ross was putting the dam in because there was money in it. But he wasn't giving ranches away to sodbusters."

Sage looked over the crowded lobby and veranda.

That evidently was the opinion of everyone who had heard the will read. The ranchers seemed very well pleased. And the homesteaders were as dejected a lot as Sage had ever seen.

John Ferris had one more question before the meeting broke up. "Where is this brother of Ross's?" he asked.

Trenton shrugged. "I don't know. I've traced him all over the country. Lost his trail in Abilene."

Sage studied the lawyer's face suspiciously. He had been in Abilene, all right. But he had not left a trail hard to follow. He had told his last employer, a rancher in southern Kansas, that he was going to Stirrup to see his brother.

He heard Ferris sigh heavily behind him. "I guess there isn't anything more we can do."

Sage suddenly held up his hand for attention. "I've got something to say before you leave."

Attention left Trenton and centered on Sage, who stood close to the door. "I'm Sage Hampton, Ross' brother."

If Sage had announced he was Billy the Kid, he wouldn't have stunned the listening crowd more. Even the lawyer standing on the desk was speechless, his mouth hanging open.

"That's not the name you gave me," Tess Brantley said finally, recovering her wits.

"I came here to see Ross," Sage explained. "When I found out he was dead, I changed my name so I could look around without being a marked man."

"But you're a saddle man," Tess said. "You won't help sodbusters."

"That's what I always thought," Sage said. "But it looks like it has been wished on me."

He turned to look over the crowd. The surprise on the faces of the homesteaders was giving away to a mixture of doubt and hope.

But there was no doubt in the faces or voices of Yake and his Circle Y riders. They were pressing toward Sage, and the shock of sudden disappointment was prodding them into an ugly mood. Sage had seen the signs before. He turned back toward those in the lobby and met the grinning freckled face of Red Hoyt.

"Thought you might need a helping hand after that charge of dynamite."

"Could be," Sage said.

Trenton had recovered now, and his shouts brought order out of a growling turmoil. "I must have proof of your identity," he shouted at Sage.

Sage pushed his way to the desk and handed a

paper he took from his shirt pocket. "That ought to do it," he said.

The crowd waited as the lawyer looked over the paper. Finally Trenton nodded. "I guess you're Sage Hampton, all right. You heard the provisions of the will?"

Sage nodded. "I did. If I want to keep the Flying H, I've got to have irrigation water running to the homesteads by October first."

"That's right," Trenton said. "Good luck. You're going to need it."

VIII

Sage and Hoyt were halted before they got past the back of the hotel by a call from one of the windows. Sage wheeled, his hand instinctively dropping to his gun. Ben Trenton was standing by an open window.

"Easy with the gun," Trenton said with a disarming grin.

"It's kind of a ticklish situation you stirred up," Hoyt said.

Trenton nodded. "Looks like it. Are you going out to the Flying H now?"

Hoyt glanced nervously up and down the alley. "With a town as hot as this one, where else would you expect us to go?"

"I'll get my horse and meet you at the edge of town," Trenton said, withdrawing his head from the window.

Sage ran a finger along his chin. "What do you make of that, Red?"

Hoyt spat disgustedly into the dust. "Looks like we're going to have a star boarder."

"Has he been out to the ranch before?" Sage asked as they hurried along the alley.

"Several times. Ross put up with him, but I don't see how."

"I take it you don't like him."

"There's no love lost on either side of the fence."

"What's wrong with him?"

"Nothing, I guess," Hoyt said as they reached the street at the end of the alley and turned toward the horses half a block away. "There are certain kinds of people I don't like, and lawyers are one of them."

They untied their horses and led them back to the alley before mounting.

They were well out of town before Ben Trenton caught up with them. He had little to say until they were almost to the Flying H.

"Think the homesteaders can hold out until they get a crop next year?" he asked when they reined up for a moment on the bluff that looked down on the homesteads to the southeast.

"They'll make it," Hoyt said. "They're no weaklings."

"You seem to be very much on their side in this dispute," Trenton said.

"Why shouldn't I be?" Hoyt demanded. "They've got a right to live, too."

"Shouldn't you be on the same side?" Sage asked the lawyer. "After all, you were Ross' lawyer, and this irrigation scheme seemed to be one of his pets."

"Of course," Trenton said quickly. "It takes a lot of people to bring civilization to a country, and that's what we must have here. I promised Ross I'd do what I could to see that the irrigation project succeeded."

At the ranch, the lawyer unrolled a pack from the back of his saddle and took down a large valise. "Which room do I get?" he asked as he came into the house.

"Same one you usually get, I reckon," Hoyt said sullenly.

"How long will he stay?" Sage asked when Trenton had gone on into his bedroom.

Hoyt shrugged. "No telling. Last time he was here over a week."

Sage put Trenton out of his mind the next morning when he left the Flying H to ride over the homesteads and decide on his next move.

He stopped at the first homestead where a roofed dugout served as a house. The other day when he had been looking for the stolen beef there had been no one there.

He swung down and started toward the door. But before he reached it, a man stepped out with a rifle cradled in his arm.

"What do you want?" he demanded.

Sage stopped, recognizing Nate Munn. Sage couldn't recall seeing Munn since the day he had tangled with him in Stirrup. His left eye still showed the effects of that battle.

"I'm just trying to find out how you feel about having irrigation here and how much effort you'd be willing to put out to get it."

"I'd like to have water," Munn said, "but not if I have to beg it from you."

"You won't be begging it from me," Sage said grimly. "You'll pay for it or you won't get it."

Munn's lips peeled back in a snarl. "That's just how I had you figured. Inside a year, you'd root us out and hog this whole flat. I don't want any part of your irrigation. Is that clear?"

"Clear enough, Munn. If the rest are like you, I won't have any trouble deciding not to put in the ditch."

"Don't come crawling to me for help on your dam,"

Munn snapped.

"You'll never see the day I'll come crawling to you for anything," Sage retorted, anger getting the better of him. "And don't expect any of the water from the ditch when it gets through."

He mounted his horse and spurred him back into the main road.

Munn was alone in his hostility. The other homesteaders welcomed Sage and gave their assurance they would help on the dam and ditch when he was ready.

At the Ferrises, he reined in and dismounted, planning to stop awhile. John Ferris met him at the door.

"Glad to see you, son," the homesteader said, motioning Sage inside. "Debbie is down at Cal's. She'll be back in a few minutes, and she'll get some dinner ready."

"I can't stop for dinner," Sage said. "I'm just making a check of the people down here to see how they feel about me taking over Ross' job and how many will help if I start work."

Ferris turned sharp eyes on Sage. "You're going to finish the dam, aren't you?"

Sage hedged. "If I want to keep the Flying H, I've got to get water down here by the first of October."

"You can depend on help from everybody down

here," Ferris said.

Sage shook his head. "I'm afraid not. Munn has already told me he wants no part of the dam."

Ferris frowned. "Nate is rather impulsive. He doesn't make friends easily. Perhaps he just hasn't had time to get acquainted with you. He'll help when you're ready for him."

"How long did Ross figure it would take him to get the dam and ditches finished?" Sage asked.

"He thought he'd have it done by the end of August. By setting the deadline at October first, he allowed you only a month to get things going again at the speed he was moving."

"You think I can make it?"

Ferris nodded slowly. "You can make it or Ross would have allowed more time. Ross was driving everybody and all his machinery hard to make it by the end of August. It's been well over a week since there has been a tap done on the dam. How much do you know about engineering?"

"Practically nothing," Sage admitted. "I've spent most of my time working cattle."

"You'll need every day between now and October to make it. You can count on help from us down here."

Sage nodded. "I'll let you know how many men I'll

need."

"Good." Ferris nodded in satisfaction. "Of course you won't need all the men on the dam at any one time. The rest will be building our church. We must get that done this year. Next year we'll be too busy with our crops to do any community building."

Sage started toward the door, then stopped as Debbie came in, followed by Cal Ufford. Ferris greeted them with a smile.

"Mr. Hampton is getting ready to resume work on the dam. He's going to need men to help."

"Then you really are going to go ahead with it?" Debbie asked in surprise.

"I'm considering it favorably," Sage said, looking sharply at Ufford.

Ufford rubbed his chin, his face expressionless. "You can count on several men from here," he said.

"I was just telling him that," Ferris said. "You can round up what he needs, can't you, Cal?"

Ufford nodded. "I reckon. But who's going to oversee the building of the church?"

"One of us will do that and the other take charge of the men who work on the dam."

"I'll ride on down the line and talk to the others," Sage said, and moved to the door.

IX

As soon as it was light the next morning, Red Hoyt was out checking the scrapers and shovels. Sage had installed him as straw boss. Before the sun was an hour high, men and teams began coming from the southeast.

Within half an hour, Hoyt had teams and scrapers bringing dirt down from the bluff and dumping it on the edge of the dike that would be the dam across the creek. A half-dozen men with shovels pushed the dirt farther out and leveled and packed it in place.

Hoyt, already sweating from a turn on the shovels, stopped by Sage, standing on the bluff overlooking the work.

"At this rate, we'll have all the dirt we want on this side of the creek in a couple of days."

"Then what?" Sage asked. He was depending on Hoyt, who had worked with Ross, knowing how to manage this construction job.

"We'll work on the other side of the creek. We'll build the dam out almost to the stream, then let it stay that way while we work on the big ditch down to the homesteads."

"How long will that take?"

Hoyt shrugged. "Hard to say. Things happened when we were working before. They'll happen again, I figure."

"Where does the trouble come from?"

Hoyt sighed. "I wish I knew. We couldn't trace it. We'd see a rider once in a while, but he was never close enough to cause the things that happened."

The first mishap came shortly after the noontime stop. A tug gave way on an old harness, and the singletree snapped back so hard it broke. Sage, who was working on the dam with a shovel, went over to the place where the scrapers were being filled with dirt.

"What caused that?" he asked the driver, a short heavy-set homesteader.

"Tug broke," he said. "I thought I had good tugs on that harness."

Sage looked at the tug. He didn't know much about harness but he saw immediately what had gone wrong. The tiny screw that held the cockeye in the tug was gone.

"That's funny," the settler said, scratching his head. "I never had one of those screws pull out before."

"Maybe it was helped," Sage suggested.

The farmer nodded. "Could be. I reckon it flew forty feet when it gave way. The team was pulling. If we could find it, we could tell."

But they couldn't find the screw, and Hoyt brought another singletree from a pile of supplies he kept in the barn. The homesteader took a heavy piece of wire and made a loop on his tug that passed for a cockeye.

It was in the middle of the following afternoon that the next breakdown occurred. This time a doubletree broke and Sage, when he investigated, found the break too smooth to be the result of natural causes.

Ferris came over to look at the accident.

"A saw has been at work here," Sage said, holding up one piece of the doubletree.

Ferris looked and finally nodded his head. "It does look like it. But who would do a thing like that?"

"A lot of people would like to see this work stopped," Sage said. "How long ago do you figure that doubletree was sawed?"

Ferris studied the piece of wood for a moment. "Not too long ago, or it would have broken it sooner."

"Could it have been done last night?"

"It could have been, I suppose," Ferris said.

Sage nodded grimly. There was sabotage. But who was doing it was another thing. He called a meeting of the workers just before quitting time that night.

"At least one of these accidents we've had was helped along by somebody," he said. "There are some people who want to stop this work. Nothing serious has happened yet, but it will if we don't stop it. I'm going to post a night guard. Red and I will take turns, but we'll need some help. Any volunteers?"

Almost the entire crew volunteered.

The guards were posted, but nothing was seen during the night. Yet things continued to happen. Two clevises broke, and they had only one in the reserve supplies. So one scraper was idle for the rest of the day.

Nate Munn had come to work the second day without a word of explanation, and Sage decided Ferris had probably called on him to fill out the crew. It settled the question in Sage's mind about the real power of Ferris among the homesteaders.

The outlet for the dam was made and the ditch started. Then Hoyt ordered the men back on the dam to bring the dirt down to the water's edge on both sides of the creek. Sage got a shock when Ufford, working with a shovel on the edge of the dirt, slipped and fell into the little stream. His scream could have been heard for a mile up and down the creek, Sage was sure. He thought that Ufford must have broken bones in the fall, but found when the lanky homesteader scrambled out of the water that a partial soaking was the extent of the damage.

"Absolutely scared to death of water," Hoyt told Sage as Ufford dried himself in the hot sun. "I'll bet he never washes his face."

Ferris was on the job the next day, looking healthier and stronger than ever. They were making a foundation for the church building, which was going to be the only frame building in the colony, and they needed more men than usual. So the crew on the dam was short-handed.

Ferris insisted on taking a hand himself and drove one of the teams on a scraper part of the time. It was after dinner that the accident happened.

Ferris was taking his turn driving and was filling his scraper, lifting up on the handle to get the blade to dig into the ground. Suddenly, as the blade began to bite into the dirt, it plunged down, throwing the handles forward with a jerk. A stronger man than Ferris might have held them down. But Ferris was jerked forward before he could release his grip on the handles. He sailed through the air, landing hard beside one of the horses.

The horses, well trained, stopped. Men close to the accident ran to Ferris. He was groaning and making no attempt to rise.

Sage was on the dam with a shovel when he heard the shout. Throwing down his shovel, he dashed up the slope to the hole at the foot of the bluff where the dirt was being dug.

"Is he hurt bad?" he asked of the first man he reached.

"Can't tell. He fell pretty hard."

Hoyt, who had been driving another team, met Sage as he got closer. "I don't think anything is broken, unless it's a collar bone," he said. "But he's jolted up pretty bad, and that isn't good for him. We'll have to take him home."

"Somebody get a rig," Sage directed, and a couple of men unhitched Ferris' team and took it to a wagon.

"I'll be all right," Ferris said. "I hurt my shoulder, that's all."

But Sage knew he wasn't all right. He considered going home with Ferris, then decided to send a couple of other men. He wanted to look into the cause of the accident.

Hoyt bent over the scraper with Sage. Sage knew what had caused the scraper to flip over as soon as he saw the blade. In the center of it was a three-inch section that curved down. The minute the scraper started to dig into the dirt, that bent place would suck almost straight down and the scraper would flip over.

"What caused that?" Hoyt said, pointing to the bent section.

"Could have been a rock, I suppose," Sage said. "But I doubt it."

He went back to the place where the scraper had flipped. There was no rock there. And the earth was no harder than at any other spot in the pit. He returned to the scraper and examined the bent spot closer.

"Looks like the work of a hammer to me," Hoyt said softly at Sage's elbow.

Sage nodded. "Just what I was thinking. Who had a chance to do that at noon?"

"There were several men around the scrapers while they ate their dinners," Hoyt said. "Some were making repairs and doing some pounding. But I didn't see anybody monkeying with the scrapers."

"Somebody did." Sage looked over the crew, trying to remember who had taken his lunch out among the scrapers that day.

While the rest of the crew went back to work, Sage walked over to the spot where the teams had been unhitched at noon. Lunch pails and sacks were placed here and there. Sage stopped suddenly where a salt sack, containing the remains of somebody's lunch, was lying on the ground. Protruding from beneath the sack was a piece of wood. Sage nudged the sack over with his toe. The wood turned out to be the handle of a hammer. And the head of the hammer was heavy.

Sage put the sack over the hammer and returned to the crew. When quitting time came, Sage moved up the slope to the spot where the teams were being unhitched from the scrapers. Somebody would claim that lunch sack, and the hammer underneath would probably belong to the owner of the sack.

He pretended to be helping to unhitch the teams as he watched. One man walked past the sack before Nate Munn came over. Munn glanced around quickly before stooping over for the sack. Then he slipped the hammer out from under the sack and inside the belt of his pants before he lifted the sack.

Sage left the team where he was working and strode over to Munn. The stocky homesteader saw him coming and turned toward his own team, which was already hitched to his wagon.

"Just a minute, Munn," Sage said.

"What do you want?" Munn demanded sourly.

"I want to ask you a question. What were you doing with that hammer today?"

"What hammer?" Munn stalled.

"The one you had hidden under your lunch sack."

"I was bending a clevis back in shape," Munn said quickly. "It spread this morning. I just dropped the hammer there with my lunch. I didn't hide it."

Sage looked at the homesteader. He was lying, Sage was sure. But the explanation Munn had given was plausible.

"I didn't see you fixing any clevis," he said.

"You don't see everything," Munn retorted.

As the homesteaders cut across the prairie toward their soddies and dugouts, Hoyt came up the slope to stand beside Sage.

"Are you going to let him get away with it?" he asked.

Sage looked at his foreman. "You saw the hammer. too?"

"I saw him pick it up just before you jumped him. I figured that was it."

"It was." Sage looked after the departing teams

"But he said he was using the hammer to straighten a clevis. I couldn't prove he wasn't."

Hoyt was looking after the wagons, too. "That looks like Munn's wagon cutting off to the north. Where do you suppose he's going?"

"I aim to find out," Sage said, striding toward the corral.

Sage clung to the creek bottom as he rode downstream. Occasionally he rode up on the meadow to make sure of Munn's location. At first Sage thought he might be going to town, but the wagon stayed south of the creek and didn't cross until it was close to the trees that surrounded Clem Yake's Circle Y headquarters.

Sage held back for about ten minutes until he saw the wagon come out of the trees and head up the north side of the creek toward Stirrup; then he rode into the Circle Y. It was dusk now, and the first lamplight in the window of the big house was burning a hole in the gathering darkness.

Clem Yake came out on the veranda of the house as Sage dismounted. "What's on your mind, Hampton?" he asked suspiciously.

"I just wanted to know what Munn was doing here."

"Munn? Do you mean Nate Munn, that dirty bulldog-faced nester?"

Sage nodded. "That's the one. I saw him drive in here just a few minutes ago."

"You crazy?" Yake came down off the porch to face Sage. "I'd shoot that greasy pig if he showed up here."

Sage studied the rancher's face for an instant. Anger twisted his features, but Sage couldn't decide how much of it was feigned.

"I saw him drive in and about ten minutes later drive out again and head for town."

"He hasn't been here," Yake shouted. "And what business would it be of yours if he had been?"

"We had a little trouble at the dam today," Sage said. "I figured Munn caused it. I thought he might be making a report."

Yake strode forward. "Get off this place, Hampton! Nobody can accuse me of hiring a sodbuster to do my dirty jobs!"

"I hope you're telling the truth, Yake," Sage said as he swung back into his saddle. "I don't figure Munn is working alone."

"I'll give you just a minute to get out of my sight," Yake bellowed.

Sage wheeled his horse and splashed across the creek.

X

August was slipping into history and the dam wasn't progressing as fast as Sage knew it should. Red Hoyt had come with the surveying instruments, and he and Sage had made an attempt to survey part of the course of the ditch. Sage was fairly well satisfied with the results.

Work on the ditch speeded up as the survey stretched out toward the homesteads. But things still happened to the machinery. Two scrapers were damaged beyond repair, and shovel handles had been broken by the dozens, it seemed to Sage. The money Ross had left to complete the dam was gone. The men were working now for free irrigation water to be given them when the water was turned in the ditch.

Then came the morning Sage and Hoyt had set to finish the survey of the ditch. Sage got his horse and waited for Hoyt to come out of the house with the instruments. But when Hoyt came out, he had only a handful of broken pieces.

"Somebody got to them. Now what do we do?"

Despair wrestled with Sage's anger. "Who could have done that?"

"Somebody must have gotten in the last day or two. We haven't been using these things, you know."

"Can we finish without those instruments?"

Hoyt shook his head. "I can't. Somebody with a perfect eye might do a fair job. But this creek isn't big enough to furnish water to waste on a bad ditch. It's all got to go to the farmers. We need another set of tools."

"There's no money to buy any more."

"I know it." Hoyt pounded a first into his hand. "But we can't finish without them. Even if we get along without the surveying outfit, we'd have to have another scraper or two. We've got a lot of dirt to move and only a month to do it."

Sage nodded, thinking hard. "We've got to have more money. And there's only one place to get it, from the homesteaders themselves."

"They don't have any money to spare."

"I know," Sage said. "But all the work they've put in so far will be wasted if we don't finish."

"Reckon you're right," Hoyt agreed. "You've got a powerful argument. How do you figure on collecting the money?"

"We'll have a meeting this afternoon at the new church building. We'll take the workers from here. Most of the others will be working on the church."

As Sage had predicted, most of the homesteaders were at the church when Sage brought those who had been working on the ditch to the meeting place. The roof was on the church building now and the men were shingling. Another two weeks, Sage guessed, would finish the job.

"I want to ask you men for some help," Sage began when all eyes turned to him. "Ross left what money he had to complete the dam and the ditch, but that is gone. Somebody got to our surveying instruments and smashed them. And two scrapers have been wrecked. We must have some more tools if we are to finish the job on time."

"Begging," Munn muttered in the silence that followed Sage's words. "He ain't satisfied with making us work like slaves. Now he wants what little money we've got."

Sage saw that Munn's resistance was reflected in more than one face. "I'm not asking you to give me your money," he said quickly. "Every dollar you put in now will be credited to you when you start paying for the water you get."

"And what if you don't finish the dam on time and lose it?" Ufford asked, pushing his way to the head of the group.

"We'll all lose," Sage said simply. "If we stop now, we know we'll lose. You men will lose all the work you've put in plus any chance you have of making a living on your homesteads. If you chip in and we get the tools and finish the job, you'll have all the water you need next summer."

Sage leaned back against the building to let the men talk it over among themselves. The murmur grew to a rumble as differences of opinion flared into arguments. Finally Ufford motioned for silence and the noise subsided.

"I'm against it," Ufford said flatly. "We agreed to help put in the dam and the ditch to get water to our crops. But we didn't agree to put in any money. We don't have money to spare. If Hampton fails to hold up his end of the bargain, we'll lose what we've already put in. But we'll still have enough money left to start somewhere else. If we give our money to Hampton, we won't have a thing left."

Some nodded; others dissented. Sage said nothing and waited.

"Look at it this way, men," Abe Masterson suddenly shouted. "We've got our homes here. We've got some of the best land in Nebraska if we can irrigate it. We've already put our work into this dam and ditch. If we don't go ahead, we'll lose a year's work and our homes. We can't lose much more by chipping in to buy the tools Hampton needs. If we get the job done, he will pay us back with water for our crops."

"Do you believe he'll really do that?" Munn sneered.

"I sure do," Masterson said positively.

Masterson's confidence in Sage began to sway the sentiments of the men. Ufford suddenly waved a hand for silence.

"Think it over," he warned. "You're giving him the money you'll need to buy grub with this winter."

"Let's ask Trenton's opinion," Masterson said quickly.

Ufford agreed. "A good idea. Ben, what do you think?"

Sage had noted that the lawyer had come along but he had forgotten him while he talked to the settlers.

"It's really none of my business," Trenton said

softly, coming forward. "But it does look like you are almost to your goal, and to throw away your chances of winning would be foolish."

His opinion was all that was needed to sway the doubtful members of the group, and when Abe Masterson called for a vote it was unanimous except for Munn and Ufford, who abstained.

Sage stepped forward. "Now I don't want any of you to run short. So chip in only what you can spare. Red will collect it, and we'll keep an account of what each man puts in. That will be credited to him. When can you have the money ready?"

"We can bring it back here tonight after we finish our chores," Masterson said. "You can't afford to waste time getting those tools."

Sage nodded. "That's right. I'll meet you here tonight and I'll get the things as soon as I can."

Sage rode close to Hoyt on the way back to work on the ditch. "Something could happen to that money just as well as to the machinery," Sage said. "After I get the money tonight, I'll go right on to Ogallala. I'll bring what I can back with me and have the heavier stuff freighted out."

"You want to ride fast and keep one hand on your gun," Hoyt warned.

"Maybe I'd better take a detour through the hills," Sage suggested.

Hoyt nodded. "I sure wouldn't ride the open trails."

Sage called an early halt to the work on the ditch so the men could go home and get the money to turn over to Sage. At the Flying H, he made preparations for the long ride to Ogallala. During an early supper, Ben Trenton brought up the subject of the trip.

"I hope you can get your tools and finish this dam soon," he said. "I've got work to do back in my office."

"Why don't you go back and tend to it?" Sage asked.

"I promised Ross I'd stick around and give you what help I could in case you were left with the task of completing the dam. At the time I gave the promise, I hardly considered the possibility of such a development. But now I feel I must live up to my promise."

"You sure take your promises seriously," Hoyt said, jamming a sagebrush root into the stove to keep the coffeepot boiling.

"I always do," Trenton said, unperturbed by Hoyt's tone. "Ross was a good friend of mine. I want to see his pet project completed."

Red Hoyt went with Sage to the church to meet the men from the homesteads. The church stood to the west of the colony on a knoll. It looked bleak and lonely in the deep dusk as Sage and his foreman rode up.

No one was there, and they dismounted to wait. In a few minutes a lone rider came from the east, straddling an awkward plow horse. Sage recognized Abe Masterson.

Hoyt frowned. "I was looking for at least a dozen of them."

Sage nodded. "So was I."

Masternson came on fast and swung off his horse before he stopped.

"Something wrong?" Sage asked quickly.

"It sure ain't all right," Masterson said.

"Didn't they chip in the money we need?" Hoyt asked.

"I've got the money," Masterson said. "But there's trouble afoot. Clem Yake rode into the settlement a little while ago. Swears another beef has been butchered. We were gathering at Ferris' to pool our money for you when he showed up. The boys tossed in their money and headed for home. Wanted to guard their places and families."

"Who was he accusing?" Sage asked, a worried frown on his face.

"Nobody in particular. But he's sure one of us settlers did it and he's out to hang somebody."

"Did you leave your wife and little girl alone?"

"They're at Ferris'. But he wouldn't hurt them. They didn't want me to make this trip. They're afraid he'll jump me because I had the fresh beef the other day. But I wanted you to get this money and get started after those tools."

"Why didn't somebody else bring it?" Hoyt demanded.

"They seemed to think Yake might try to burn their homes."

"Can't burn sod," Hoyt snorted.

"He could burn the furniture," Sage said. "But I don't believe he'd do anything like that. You'd better keep your eye peeled, though, Abe. Did Yake find out what you were doing?"

"I don't know," Masterson said. "But we were counting the money when he came, so I imagine he can guess what's up."

"That could mean trouble for you, Sage," Hoyt said.

Sage nodded. "I reckon, although there is no proof that Yake is behind our trouble."

"No proof that he ain't, either," Hoyt retorted.

Masterson drew a little bag from his pocket. "Here is three hundred and fifty dollars we collected," he said. "It's all in gold, mostly double eagles. Debbie has a list of how much each man put in. Will this be enough?"

Sage nodded as he took the bag and emptied it into the money belt he was wearing for the trip. "More than enough, I think. This should buy the tools we need and the material to build the gate in the main ditch."

"I'll be getting back then," Masterson said, glancing nervously down toward the homesteads.

"Sure," Sage said. "I hope Yake doesn't cause you folks any trouble."

"We'll make out. Good luck, Sage."

Masterson kicked his horse into a lope and disappeared into the deepening darkness. Sage and Hoyt stood in silence as the homesteader's horse pounded away.

"Do you think you ought to start tonight?" Hoyt asked finally. "Yake will expect you to, if he knows what's up."

"If I wait it will just give him more of a chance to ambush me."

"I reckon." Hoyt started to say more, then held up his hand, cocking a listening ear.

Sage had heard it, too: the distant drum of hoofbeats. With Hoyt, he listened as the beats grew slower, then stopped.

"What do you make of that?" Hoyt asked in a low tone.

Sage shook his head. "I don't know. It wasn't Masterson. Sounded to me like it was off to the northwest."

"It was," Hoyt said. "Somebody riding. That could mean anything or nothing. Could have been some homesteader out after a cow he had staked a long way from home, or some Circle Y or TS rider."

"Probably was," Sage said. "We're pretty jumpy. That horse could have been quite a way off, too. Sound carries a long way tonight."

"Why doesn't he move on?" Hoyt asked after a moment's attentive listening.

"He probably is moving at a walk now. We wouldn't hear that."

Hoyt sighed. "Well, if you're going tonight, you'd better get started. It's a long way to Ogallala."

Sage nodded, knowing what Hoyt was thinking. "And I may need all the head start I can get."

"Could be," Hoyt said. "Good luck."

Sage mounted and turned his horse straight south into the sandhills.

He rode at a trot for half a mile, cutting a little east as he went. He paused every few minutes to listen. The first couple of times he heard nothing; then when he stopped the third time, he caught a sound behind him. Dismounting, he knelt and pressed an ear to the ground. There was no mistaking the soft thump of hoofbeats. The horse was moving at a walk and wasn't too far away.

For five minutes he rode slowly, listening for sound of pursuit. There was no moon, and high clouds blotted out most of the stars. If his pursuer hadn't heard his horse veer to the north, it was likely that he had lost the trail completely.

He paused again and dismounted, laying an ear to the ground. For a minute he held his breath and heard nothing. Then, just as he was about to rise, he heard the soft stamp of a horse's hoof. He guessed the horse wasn't over fifty yards away. His rider evidently was aware of every move Sage was making.

Sage peered into the blackness behind him, his hand on his gun. But there was nothing visible there. He mounted again. If he could get to the settlement, he'd cache the money at Ferris' for the night and start for Ogallala tomorrow. There was no question in Sage's mind but that his pursuer was after that money.

He rode half turned in the saddle, watching his back-trail. But he wasn't prepared for the stab of the knife that struck him in the lower part of his shoulder. He twisted in the saddle as pain shot through his body, and saw the rider. He had come up on Sage's right side while Sage was looking over his left shoulder.

But he couldn't identify the man, for horse and rider were beginning to blur before his eyes and he had to grab the saddle horn to keep from falling. He kicked his horse into a run, bending low over the saddle. His right arm was useless, slapping against his gun which he couldn't use.

Faintly he heard the other rider coming after him and concentrated on staying in the saddle. His hands felt big and numb and the saddle horn seemed to be swelling under his fingers. Blood ran down his back and pain swept over him till it brought a muffled cry to his lips. Then a welcome blackness enveloped him, shutting out the pain. He tried to hold the saddle horn, but it grew too big for his fingers to grip. He knew he was falling, but it didn't matter any more. . . .

The sun was shining brightly when Sage roused from unconsciousness. There was a dull ache in his back, and he was sick. Memory came back, and he struggled to a sitting position. He felt first for the money belt with the three hundred and fifty dollars Abe Masterson had given him. It was gone.

XI

Debbie found it hard to dispel the uneasiness that had invaded the settlement when Clem Yake had appeared with the accusation that someone had butchered another of his steers.

Morning brought no relief. All through breakfast and the morning chores, she tried to fight off a premonition of disaster. And when Abe Masterson galloped into the yard about nine o'clock, she was sure his news would be bad. She opened the door for him and stepped back, knowing he would want to report his father.

John Ferris was sitting in his rocking chair. He leaned forward when he saw Masterson, worry lines creasing his forehead. "Is something wrong, Abe?"

"Everything's wrong," Masterson said. "I've just come from Hampton's. Sage's horse came in sometime last night with blood on the saddle."

"Where's Sage?" Debbie demanded before her father could speak.

"Nobody knows. Hoyt has gone out to look for him."

"Did he start for Ogallala last night?"

Masterson nodded. "He was ready to leave when I gave him the money last night at the church. It seemed to worry him when he found out Clem Yake had been here."

Ferris nodded thoughtfully. "Did he think Yake might try to take the money from him?"

"He asked me if Yake knew we were collecting money for him. I reckon he figured the ranchers are behind all the trouble we've been having with the dam. And I think he's right. If Yake did figure out what we were doing here last night, he'd try to get that money from Sage. That would stop the dam."

Ferris sank his chin in his hand, and Debbie turned thoughtfully to the window, her mind on Sage and the money the homesteaders had collected for him.

She sighed and turned back to Masterson. "What will we do now?"

"Cal is calling a meeting for noon today," Masterson said. "We'll talk it over then."

"Where are they going to have the meeting?" Ferris asked.

"Right here. We wanted you to be there."

"If our money is gone," Debbie said hopelessly,

"there isn't much we can do about it."

"Cal thinks there is. And I agree with him. We can't just sit down and do nothing."

Ferris nodded. "That's right. But we mustn't be too hasty in our judgments or actions. Cal is a trifle impulsive. Did he say what he intends to do?"

"No," Masterson said. "He's rounding up everybody now. Whatever he's got in mind, he wants every man in the colony to know about it."

"Maybe he wants to try to raise more money," Ferris suggested.

Masterson shook his head. "It won't be that. He was against raising what we did yesterday. He's got other ideas that are pushing him hard."

Masterson left, saying he'd be back by noon or before. Debbie picked some string beans out of her garden and got them ready for dinner, but she wasn't thinking about her work.

Noon came, and she and her father ate an early dinner so as to be ready for the meeting that was to follow. Neighbors began coming in shortly after noon, and by the time Debbie had all the dishes washed and put in the cupboard, the house was half full.

Cal Ufford was one of the last to arrive. He stalked in, a heavy scowl on his face as he looked over the roomful of men.

"Everybody here?" he asked.

"I think so," Ferris said. "What's the purpose of the meeting, Cal?"

"There are some things to decide," Ufford said. "We've got to take things in our own hands if we intend to survive here."

"We've been working on the dam and digging the irrigation ditch," one homesteader said. "What else can we do?"

"Do the bossing ourselves," Ufford snapped. "We let Hampton tell us he needed tools, though we're not even sure he did. But we dug up the money and gave it to him, and now tell me where it is."

Masterson asked, "Do you think Hampton made off with our money?"

"What else do you think happened to it?"

"Somebody stole it," Masterson said quickly; "probably Clem Yake. He was here last night while we were getting the money ready to take to Hampton."

"That's a good excuse for Hampton."

"But there was blood on Hampton's saddle when the horse came in last night," Ferris objected.

Ufford nodded. "There was. A gunman like Hampton would have little trouble killing a rabbit or prairie chicken and sprinkling some blood on his saddle. He could have had another horse staked out somewhere. By now he's probably fifty miles from here."

Another settler spoke up, the frown on his face proof that he wasn't convinced. "But we know those scrapers were broken. Somebody was causing all that trouble."

"Sure the scrapers were damaged beyond repair," Ufford said. "But who had access to those tools every night? I'll tell you. Sage Hampton. You all know he sided with the ranchers when he first came here. He admits being a saddle man. And you never saw a saddle man who sympathized with homesteaders."

"But he'll lose the Flying H if he doesn't get the dam and ditch done by the first of October," Masterson argued.

"That's what the will says. But I'll tell you what I think. Hampton knows who will get that ranch if he fails to meet those provisions. Whoever it is had probably offered Hampton a good price if he fails to meet the deadline. By slowing work on the ditch and then bleeding us for three hundred and fifty dollars in addition to what he was paid for the ranch, he's making out pretty good."

Debbie saw in many of the faces a willingness to believe Ufford. But still there was doubt in a few.

Masterson was one of the doubters.

"There's no proof that Hampton skipped out with our money," he said.

"Does the theory that somebody stole it from him sound more reasonable than that Hampton should run off with it and clean up a small fortune on the whole setup?"

"It does to me," Masterson said.

Ufford whirled on the others. "What about you? I say we ought to get on Hampton's trail and bring our money back."

Heads nodded, and Masterson suddenly agreed. "You're right, Cal. That's the only way we can find out what really happened to Hampton.. He headed south into the hills from the church."

"Why?" Ufford shot at him.

"To avoid any ambush which might be set for him along the regular trail east from here."

"When we find him, we ought to hang him from a wagon tongue," Munn said savagely.

"I'd like to say a word," John Ferris said, and silence dropped over the room like a mantle. "I think we're being too hasty in our condemnation of Sage Hampton. After all, we have no proof that he is guilty. And we should believe him innocent until proven guilty."

Silence held the room for a long minute. Then Ufford spoke again. "That's what I'd like to do. But we can't sit around with folded hands while he gets farther away. We need that money he got away with, and we need it bad."

Again heads nodded, but Ferris stopped them with a raised hand. "I'm inclined to believe Sage Hampton is honest. I don't doubt that our money is gone, but I don't think Hampton stole it. I'm against any rash move until we know for certain that he is guilty."

Ufford objected, but Debbie watched sentiment quickly swing in favor of John Ferris' position.

When the meeting had broken up, after Ufford had succeeded in getting three men to look for Sage's trail, Debbie went out to saddle her horse. She wanted some time to think about what she had heard.

She headed her horse for the lookout hill where she loved to go when she had a problem to work out. Halfway across the level prairie to the hills that rimmed the valley, she saw a rider to her right and thought she recognized Tess Brantley. Wondering what the TS owner would be doing there, she reined her horse to the west to intercept the other rider.

When Tess saw Debbie, she stopped and waited.

"Haven't seen anything of a half-dozen TS cows, have you?" Tess asked. "I thought they might have wandered into the hills."

Debbie shook her head. "Haven't seen them. But then I haven't been riding much lately. I've been taking care of Daddy."

"I heard he got hurt. Too bad. I also heard you were going to be married soon. Anything to that?"

"I am," Debbie said defensively. "I'm getting a wonderful man."

Tess shrugged. "I hope things turn out well for you." She lifted her reins. "Sometime when you happen by the TS, stop in and I'll give you some lace I have. It would make a pretty trimming for your wedding gown."

And Tess rode off at a gallop.

At the lookout, Debbie dismounted, her mind on the problem facing the homesteaders. But she forgot that problem the instant she looked down at her feet.

There was a patch of dried blood the size of a plate on the grass. Instantly she thought of Sage.

Her eyes swept the hilltop, trying to pick up a bloody trail on the parched grass. She found one spot to the south and another to the west near the little gully that separated the lookout from a smaller knoll.

She followed the bloody trail to the south a way until she lost it, then came back and did the same with the one to the west. She knew that the hot sun would be too much for a wounded man. But when she failed to find any trace of Sage in the gully except for another small pool of dried blood, she went back to her horse in despair.

She was about to mount, intending to circle around the area in hopes of picking up more signs, when she saw another rider coming straight for the knoll. He was holding a course along the edge of the sandhills, coming from the direction of the Flying H.

As he came nearer she recognized Ben Trenton, the lawyer. He looked smaller than ever in the saddle of a big horse. He reined up beside Debbie, wearing a wide smile.

"It's a pleasant surprise finding you here," he said.

"Have they found Sage?" Debbie asked.

"I don't know," Trenton said. "I haven't been at the ranch since this morning. I've been looking for Sage myself. It seems he has just vanished."

Debbie looked sharply at the lawyer. "What do you mean by that?"

"Just that we can't find him," Trenton said. "Seems odd that we can't find at least what's left of him, if he ran into foul play."

"Do you think there's any doubt of that?"

Trenton was thoughtful for a moment. "No. It's almost certain that somebody must have overtaken him and robbed him. No telling what else they did to him."

"Do you think he's been killed?"

The lawyer sighed. "It's quite possible. Sage had a lot of opposition to the building of that dam, you know. Some people would rather see him dead than alive."

"Where are you going to look now?"

Trenton waved an arm to the south. "Through the hills again. But I feel like taking a rest right now." He swung down and stepped over close to Debbie. "You know, Debbie, you're too pretty to be wasting your time on Cal Ufford."

Surprised, Debbie backed away from the lawyer. "Please, Mr. Trenton, don't say things like that."

The lawyer laughed softly. "No harm in telling the truth, is there? You're the prettiest girl this side of the Missouri."

She moved farther away from him, backing into her horse. He laughed again and caught her arm. "Don't be afraid of me."

Debbie struck at him, but he only laughed and

tightened his grip. Just then she caught a glimpse of a rider pounding up the hill from the settlement. Trenton heard the approaching rider and wheeled to face him, his hand slipping inside his coat in a significant move.

Debbie, looking at the newcomer, breathed easier when she saw it was Cal Ufford. Jerking his horse to a halt, Ufford swung down and in three long strides was facing Trenton.

"What's the idea, Ben?" he demanded.

Trenton laughed, but Debbie thought she detected a note of uneasiness in the sound. "I was just talking to Debbie."

"What about?"

"Private business," Trenton said. "I was telling her how pretty she was. Going to deny that?"

Ufford frowned, but suddenly he seemed to have lost most of his belligerence. "You're moving in on territory that doesn't belong to you," he said.

"I'm going home, Cal," Debbie said.

Ufford nodded. "That's a good idea." He turned to Trenton again, ignoring Debbie. "Now you'd better get some things straight."

Debbie didn't wait for any more. She heard Trenton's laugh as she kicked her horse into a lope toward the settlement.

XII

Sage remembered nothing from the time he lost consciousness until he opened his eyes in a small bedroom. After careful concentration to bring his mind into focus, he recognized the room as his own.

The door to his room opened a crack and Red Hoyt peeked in.

"Come on in here," Sage demanded in a weak voice.

"Last time I looked in I thought you were asleep," Hoyt said. "Now you take it easy. Doc said he'd ride out tonight and take a look at you."

"How did I get here?"

"I brought you," Hoyt said, seating himself on the edge of the bed. "When your horse came in with blood on the saddle, I took out on your trail. Found you just a little after noon in a gully southwest of the homesteads."

"Didn't find the money, did you?"

Hoyt shook his head. "Whoever tossed that knife into you got away with the money. That was what he was after, I suppose."

"What do we do now?"

Hoyt sighed. "First you've got to get on your feet."

"What about the work on the dam?"

"I don't know," Hoyt said. "The settlers had a meeting this afternoon. I saw Abe Masterson when I went in to get Doc Merrick. Abe said some of the settlers thought you ran off with the money. I told him what happened. But I doubt if they'll have any more money to put into tools. And I can't see how we can finish without tools."

"We've got to finish it somehow, Red," Sage said grimly.

"I didn't think you were so dead set on the idea."

"I wasn't at first," Sage admitted. "But when they try to stop me with a knife, it puts things in a different light. I'm going to lick them, whoever they are, if I can."

"The odds are pretty heavy against us," Hoyt said. "I'll see what the homesteaders think about it now."

"You can finish the dam with the scrapers we have," Sage said. "We'll get the tools to finish the ditch before the deadline."

Hoyt walked to the door. "You'll finish yourself if you don't shut up and get some rest."

Hoyt went outside, and the long afternoon dragged on. The doctor came and examined Sage and nodded in satisfaction.

"That's a mighty good job of cleaning that cut," he said to Hoyt, who had come in with him. "Doesn't look like any infection. The worst thing that happened to him was a loss of blood."

"How long will I be here, Doc?" Sage asked.

The doctor looked at Sage. "That depends on how you behave. Three or four days if you take it easy. You can be back at easy work in ten days maybe."

"No maybe about it," Sage said. "I've got to be."

"If you get out of there too soon," the doctor warned, "you'll open up that wound and you'll be back in that bed for a month."

Sage remained quiet for three days mainly because he didn't feel like doing anything else. On the fourth day he felt so much stronger that he persuaded Hoyt to help him sit on the edge of the bed. Only then did he realize how weak he was. A few minutes on the edge of the bed and he was willing to lie down and stay there.

But his strength returned quickly, and within a week he was moving around the house almost as he pleased. The doctor had been back once and pronounced everything fine.

A couple of nights later Sage announced to Hoyt that he was going out the next day to see how work was progressing.

"Better take it easy," Hoyt cautioned. "We're doing all right. Some of the settlers won't come back to work, figuring they're just wasting their time. But enough of them have been here so that we'll finish the dam in a couple of days. We've got the spillway all finished, and we're plagging the center of the dam now."

Sage drummed his fingers on the table. "If we just had the tools we need to finish that ditch, we could still make it by the deadline."

Hoyt nodded. "I reckon we could. But we've got to have money. Think you could borrow any at the bank?"

"I doubt it," Sage said. "I've been trying to figure out who could have taken that money belt from me."

"Even if you knew, you couldn't get it back."

"If I knew, I'd make a good try. Trenton isn't here now, is he?"

Hoyt shook his head. "He went to town this afternoon and hasn't come back yet. I don't care if he never comes. You don't think he had anything to do with it, do you?"

"I'm not sure," Sage said thoughtfully. "He was the only one besides Masterson who knew I was going to start to Ogallala that night."

Hoyt nodded, his face brightening. "That's right. He heard us make the plans. He could be the one."

"It could have been Clem Yake, too," Sage said. "He had plenty of reason to try to stop me. And he might have guessed what I was up to."

"Could have been," Hoyt agreed. "And if either one of those jaspers got it, we won't get it back."

Sage sighed. "Probably not. I'll be glad when I can get out there and do something. I'm going crazy here."

He was out at the dam most of the next day and was well pleased with himself that he didn't tire too quickly. The next day he also spent with the workers and even took a hand in the work.

That night as he and Hoyt planned the next day's work, a rider came into the yard. A knock on the door brought them both alert.

"I'll get it," Hoyt said, pushing back his chair.

Sage waited. He wasn't prepared for the visitor who came in when Hoyt opened the door.

Tess Brantley wasted no words in salutation. "Is Ben Trenton here?" she asked.

Sage shook his head. "He went to town this morning. At least that's where he said he went."

"No telling where he really went," Tess said.

There was an edge to her words that made Sage look at her closely. "I take it this wasn't to be a friendly call on Trenton."

Tess accepted the chair Hoyt pulled up for her. "It was business. But I might have known I wouldn't catch him. He always manages to be somewhere else when he's wanted."

"What's he done to you?" Hoyt asked.

Tess shrugged. "Forget I even mentioned him. I suppose I might as well get back to the TS."

"What's the hurry?" Sage said. "It isn't often we have company; at least company we enjoy."

"It sure ain't," Hoyt added enthusiastically.

"I guess there isn't any great rush," Tess agreed, settling back in her chair. "I hear you stopped a knife in the back, Sage. I wasn't expecting to find you on your pins yet."

Sage grinned. "My hide's pretty tough. But the money I had is gone."

"Any idea who took it?"

Sage nodded. "Idea, yes. But nothing to get my teeth in. Clem Yake was down at Ferris' the night the settlers gathered the money for me. He might have figured out what was in the wind and waylaid me."

Tess shook her head. "I doubt it. You got that knife in the back, didn't you?"

"Right under the shoulder blade," Sage said.

"Then it wasn't Yake," Tess said positively. "In the first place, he wouldn't use a knife; he'd use a gun. In the second place, he'd make sure you were facing him when he pulled the trigger. Who else do you suspect?"

"I didn't say I suspected anyone," Sage said cautiously. "But Trenton was the only man who knew my plan."

Tess studied the faces of the two men. "Don't you trust him?" she asked finally.

"I don't," Hoyt said positively.

"Do you know Ben Trenton well?" Sage asked her.

Tess shrugged. "He's been here before. As for suspecting him of robbing you, that's the smartest idea you've had."

"You think he might have done it?" Hoyt asked quickly.

"If he knew you were going to have a lot of money

with you, I'd lay odds he did it."

Sage sighed. "Thinking he took the money and getting it back are two different things."

"I can't say that I want you to get that money back," Tess said, "but I hate to see a dog like Trenton get away with it. I could tell you how to get it from him."

Sage leaned forward, studying Tess' face intently. "Do you know where he put it?"

"I'd give you two to one odds I could find it. Every penny he owns is in a money belt he wears every waking hour. He doesn't trust any bank. He thinks they are as crooked as he is."

"We could hold him up and see," Hoyt suggested.

"There's an easier way," Tess said eagerly. "He'll take off his money belt and hang it over a chair right by his bed at night."

Sage frowned. "How do you know so much about his habits?"

She smiled a little, and then her face went grim again. "I know a lot of things no one ever guesses I do. The important thing for you, it seems to me, is to get that money back."

Sage nodded. "You're right. We'll make a try."

She got to her feet. "I think I'll be riding. No telling when Trenton will get here. I'll see him later."

Sage watched her go, and he and Hoyt listened to the drumming hoofbeats of her horse fade into the night. Then Hoyt sighed and turned to Sage.

"What do you make of her?"

"Either she knows more about Ben Trenton than anyone else in this end of the state, or that was a nice juicy trap."

Trenton rode in before Sage had gotten to sleep. Sage didn't find it hard to stay awake for another half-hour after the lawyer came into the house. Then, long after everything was still, he crawled out of bed. He found Hoyt already up.

"Who's going to take a look?" Hoyt whispered.

"I will," Sage said. "You back me up."

Hoyt patted the gun in his hand. "I didn't bring this along just because I'm nervous."

They moved silently through the living room to the door of Trenton's bedroom. For a long minute Sage listened to the even breathing of the lawyer, then quietly turned the knob on the door.

The door opened softly, and Sage stood there, his eyes trying to pierce the darkness and finally succeeding enough to make out Trenton in the bed and a chair pulled up against the bed.

Silently he tiptoed into the room. He could hear

Hoyt breathing behind him and motioned for him to stay out of the room. Close to the chair now, he discovered two moneybelts draped over the back.

Sage lifted one of the belts off the chair, keeping an eye on the quiet figure in the bed. The belt was heavy and had a familiar feel to it, but it was too dark to identify it. He backed carefully out of the room and pulled the door quietly shut behind him.

"Get it?" Hoyt whispered.

"I got one," Sage answered. "There were two."

They crossed to Sage's room and lit his lamp. Hoyt whistled softly when Sage poured a handful of eagles and double eagles on the bed. Sage glanced at the money, then examined the belt carefully.

"This is the belt I was wearing, all right," he said softly. "Wonder if the three hundred and fifty is all here."

A quick count proved that it was. Hoyt looked at it and scratched his chin. "I can't quite figure how Tess knew so much about Trenton. She called the turn exactly."

Sage nodded. "Couldn't have been any nearer exact if Trenton had been in on it."

"Think he was?" Hoyt asked.

Sage shook his head. "I can't imagine Trenton deliberately letting us get this money back. He's not built that way. He'll be tearing his hair in the morning when he finds this money belt is gone."

Hoyt grinned. "I just hope he says something about it. I've got a lot of questions to ask him. Are you going to string him up or tar and feather him?"

"Neither now," Sage said. "I'll settle with him later when I have time. Right now I'm heading for Ogallala for those tools."

"Tonight?"

Sage nodded. "Trenton won't follow me with a knife this time, because he doesn't even know I've got the money. If I waited till morning, it would be different."

"You're right," Hoyt agreed. "By morning you'll be so far away Trenton won't be able to do anything about it. I'll keep an eye on that jasper till you get back. He won't cause you any trouble on the way home, either."

Sage grinned. "I won't worry about Trenton. I'll be back with what tools I can carry on my saddle day after tomorrow."

XIII

Sage was back with the surveying equipment by the time he had set. The bigger pieces such as scrapers and the gate for the irrigation ditch were being hauled down by a freighter Sage had hired in Ogallala.

Without taking any time for rest, Sage went with Hoyt to continue the survey of the ditch. By noon they had enough of the ditch staked out so that a crew of workers could begin digging. Sage rode down to Ferris'.

Hoyt had spread the word that the money had been recovered and that Sage had gone for the tools. Ferris, almost fully recovered from his accident, came out to meet Sage when he rode up.

"Ready to go to work again?" he asked.

Sage nodded. "Red and I got some surveying done this morning. We could use a crew this afternoon."

"We'll have the men there," Ferris promised. "The

church is done now. The dedication is Sunday. You'll be there, won't you?"

Sage hesitated. "I'd like to be," he said. "I don't know how my work will be coming by then."

"You'll never lose anything by resting one day in seven," Ferris said. "I hope you'll come. We'll have regular services in the morning and a picnic lunch at noon. There will be a special program in the afternoon."

Debbie appeared in the doorway behind her father. "You must come," she urged. "We want everybody in the country there."

Sage grinned. "I'll be there if I can make it. But if everybody in the country is there, we might see some fireworks."

"There'll be peace in the Lord's house that day," Ferris promised.

The homesteaders turned out for the afternoon's work, the biggest crew Sage had had since taking over Ross' pet project. The work went along rapidly.

Sage and Hoyt finished the survey to the first homestead that afternoon. As Hoyt pointed out, it was the only smart thing to do. All the other surveying equipment had been smashed before they could finish the work, so they had to complete the job this time before anyone had a chance to wreck the tools.

On his way home, Sage examined the work done. It had progressed farther than he had expected, but when he checked the advance of the ditch against the calendar, he realized that it wasn't enough.

"We won't make it," Hoyt said solemnly, looking over Sage's shoulder at the calendar.

"Looks that way," Sage said, dropping in a chair with a sigh. "But all we can do is try."

"We might make a shallower ditch and get through faster," Hoyt suggested.

Sage shook his head. "We're making it as shallow as we dare to now. If the ditch doesn't hold water we'll fail just the same. We'll go as fast as we can and hope we can make it."

But by Saturday night, it was becoming obvious that the ditch wouldn't be finished in time. None of the homesteaders was going to work on Sunday. Everything would stop for the dedication. Sage knew he should go, too, if he intended to stay in the good graces of the settlers.

Sage went to Stirrup the first thing Sunday morning. He had some unfinished business with Ben Trenton. Trenton hadn't been at the Flying H since Sage had gotten back from Ogallala. Yet Masterson had told

Sage he had seen Ben in Stirrup twice.

But though he searched the entire town and asked questions of everyone he saw, he found no trace of Trenton. Most of the townspeople were either going or were already on their way to the church for the dedication ceremonies.

Finally Sage gave up his search and followed the crowd to the church on the west side of the homesteader settlement. Church services were almost over when he slipped into the door and stood along the back wall.

There was a small platform at the other end of the church, and the pulpit stood on one end of it. John Ferris was behind the pulpit now, preaching. On the other end of the platform was a choir with a dozen singers. An organ sat on the floor in front of the singers. Sage caught a glimpse of Debbie in the choir.

When the sermon was over and the choir had sung a closing song, the people filed out into the treeless yard.

Food was brought from the wagons and placed on a dozen tablecloths the women had spread together on the ground. Sage thought he had never seen so much to eat. And these were the people who would starve before next summer unless he got that irrigation water to them!

The food was plain but it was good. Sage felt out of place, for he hadn't brought his share. But Debbie came to him where he stood on the outer fringes of the crowd, and she had a plate and fork and spoon.

"Here," she said, handing him the plate. "Get in line. You're Daddy's and my guest today."

He grinned. "Thanks. Looks like there will be enough for everybody, all right."

"We live simply but we live well," she said, and pulled him over to the line of men forming at one end of the huge picnic spread.

John Ferris, excitement flushing his pale face, checked his watch after a while, then rang the bell that was hanging in the steeple. Dishes clattered as they were hurriedly put away, and the food still on the tablecloths disappeared as if by magic. Sage hunted up Debbie, gave her his empty plate and thanked her for the dinner. In five minutes all signs of the huge picnic dinner were gone and the people were filing back into the church for the dedication program.

There weren't enough seats in the church for the crowd and Sage contented himself with a spot along the back wall. Hoyt had come for the afternoon program and leaned back against the wall beside Sage.

While the crowd was singing, accompanied by the

mellow tones of the organ, Sage looked over the roomful of people, trying to locate some of the ranchers. The only rancher he saw was Tess Brantley in the row of seats just ahead of Sage. Hoyt had already seen her, Sage discovered, for he was staring at the back of her head.

Sage grinned and nudged his foreman. "Kind of pretty, isn't she?"

Hoyt jumped and flushed like a youngster caught in the cookie jar. "She sure is," he said softly.

"Maybe she likes redheads; who knows?"

Hoyt shook his head. "Not if he's putting in an irrigation ditch for these settlers."

The singing stopped, and Sage could say no more in the silence that followed. Ferris took command again, and Sage saw the pride in him as he spoke. This was the culmination of his dream.

After the program, Sage waited close to the door of the church, reluctant to leave the peacefulness he had found there. A dozen of the homesteaders spoke to him and invited him to the regular Sunday morning services which would begin the following Sunday.

Debbie made the rounds, speaking to all she could. But Cal Ufford stopped her just before she reached Sage.

"I've got some business I have to attend to in town, Debbie," he said apologetically. "I hate to run off, but you can go home with your father. I'll see you tomorrow."

"Of course, Cal," Debbie said, watching him with a puzzled frown as he turned away.

Sage got a moment of satisfaction from knowing Ufford wasn't going to take her home today.

While he was berating himself for being a jealous fool, John Ferris hurried up to Debbie.

"I've invited Dillon home with us for supper, Debbie. I can't leave here till everybody goes home. Could you take the rig and go on and get supper started? I'll come with Dillon."

Sage knew that Dillon ran the hardware store in town. He had seen him and several other townspeople out there today. The next instant another thought struck him, and he acted on it impulsively.

"Mind if I drive you home, Debbie?" he asked.

For an instant she looked startled; then she smiled. "Why, no, of course not, Sage."

He chided himself for feeling like a fuzzy-cheeked boy on his first date as he led Debbie out to Ferris' little road cart. Only a few rigs remained now, among them Dillon's surrey. Getting his horse, Sage tied him behind the road cart and turned the rig toward the settlement to the east.

"That was a fine program," Sage said when they were heading down the slope.

"It was good, wasn't it? It's been the biggest day of Daddy's life."

"Getting that ditch done should mean even more to him."

She nodded, the radiance leaving her face. "I suppose it should. It's a good thing there are practical people in the world, I guess. Sometimes I think Daddy is too idealistic. But it's wonderful to be like Daddy and not hate or distrust anyone."

"I reckon it would be," Sage admitted slowly. "You're like him, aren't you?"

"I try to be. I don't know of anyone I dislike."

"Not even me?" Sage said, and he knew his voice was giving away more than his words were saying.

"I like you, Sage. You know that." She laid a hand on his arm as he started to speak. "Don't, Sage. I don't want to have to say anything that will hurt you."

He looked at Debbie with new eyes. She was only a girl, barely twenty, yet she had the insight of a mature woman. His admiration for her went up another notch.

"I can name a lot of things that are wrong with me," he said slowly. "But what are your objections?"

She folded her hands in her lap and looked down at them. "You won't be angry if I tell you?"

He grinned wryly. "I'm asking for it. I won't have any grounds for getting mad."

She looked at him. "Maybe it isn't your fault, Sage, but you're not a religious man. You seem to think religion is a superstition meant for weak minds and old fogies."

He swallowed hard.

"Maybe I once felt like that, Debbie. But knowing people like you and Abe Masterson has made me change my mind."

"I wish we could change your mind completely. There's no happier life than one of love and peace."

Sage nodded slowly. "I agree with that. But it's hard to accomplish. And if I did change my mind?"

She bit her underlip. "You know I'm going to marry Cal Ufford the first of October, don't you?"

He caught his breath. He had heard the two names linked together often, but he hadn't supposed it had reached this stage. "No," he said flatly. "Why Ufford?" He realized it was a stupid question the instant he had asked it.

She stiffened. "Cal is a good man and the man of my choice."

He couldn't keep from saying, "Don't you mean the man of your father's choice?"

She bit her lip again, but no angry words came. She said only, "Was that fair?"

"I'm sorry, Debbie," he said.

Silence built up a barrier between them as the road cart rolled over the new road and finally stopped in front of the barn at Ferris' soddy. Sage wished a dozen times that he had minded his own business and ridden straight back to the Flying H. Debbie had made it embarrassingly plain that that was where he belonged.

"I'll get supper started," Debbie said. "Will you put the horse away?"

"Of course," he said readily.

She stepped out of the cart. "You'll stay for supper, too, won't you?"

He was surprised at the invitation but knew he couldn't accept. He could have but one purpose in staying, and Debbie had already made it plain that that goal was out of his reach. A rider pounding in from the east saved him the embarrassment of refusing.

Both he and Debbie turned to face the rider, and

Sage recognized Nate Munn before he pulled his horse to a stop. Excitement brightened the man's surly features.

"Circle Y cattle broke into Abe's cornfield this afternoon and ruined his whole crop," Munn reported.

Sage came around the cart. "How do you know?"

"I just came from there," Munn said. "Abe's headed for the Circle Y now."

"It won't do any good to talk to Yake," Debbie said. "Doesn't Abe know that?"

"Abe's pretty mad," Munn said. "Figures on making Yake pay for the damage done to his corn."

"Yake won't do that," Debbie said, worry raising the pitch of her voice. "There'll be trouble." She looked at Sage.

"I'll ride over to the Circle Y and see what I can do," Sage said.

"Please hurry." Debbie's eyes thanked him. "I'll take care of the horse."

Sage didn't wait to see if Munn would offer to help Debbie. If Abe Masterson had already headed for the Circle Y, he'd be there before Sage could make it.

The road took him close to Masterson's cornfield, and Sage saw where the fence had been torn down and the field badly torn up.

Sage wanted to look at the wire to see if it had been cut, but he didn't have time for that now. He wondered about Munn. Then he realized that Munn hadn't been responsible, for he recalled seeing the surly homesteader and Masterson leaving the church together that afternoon. Munn had probably been with Masterson when they had discovered the damage to the crop.

Sage cut across the prairie toward the Circle Y. Masterson's horse was in the yard at Yake's ranch, and Sage saw the lean farmer standing at the hitchrack shouting angrily at Clem Yake, who was pacing the veranda.

Sage pounded into the yard and pulled up beside Masterson's horse, but he didn't dismount. He looked from one man to the other, trying to decide how far tempers had been stretched. Trouble here would not only be disastrous to the settlers and the ranchers, but it would kill what little hope Sage still had of completing the irrigation ditch before the deadline.

Yake stopped his pacing and scowled at Sage. "What's your put-in?" he roared.

"I'm not sure yet," Sage said, leaning an elbow on the saddle horn. "I came over to see if I could keep you two hotheads from chewing each other up."

"All I'm asking is that he pay for the damage his

cattle did to my cornfield," Masterson said, a clenched fist pounding the hitchrack.

"He can't even prove my cattle were in his corn," Yake shouted. "Anyway, if he can't protect his stuff, that's not my fault."

"I've got a good rifle," Masterson said hotly. "Next time I'll kill a few head in the field. Maybe you'll believe they're yours then."

Yake shook a fist at Masterson. "You kill one of my cattle and I'll come over there and burn you to the ground."

Sage recognized the roll of thunder which heralded a coming storm. "Now you'd both better cool off," he said sharply. "The way you're pawing the ground, you're going to start something you can't stop. Abe, you go home."

Masterson scowled at Sage, and Yake started to swear. Sage turned on him with a sharp, "Shut up." For a moment Yake stared in amazement at Sage; then he roared like a wounded bull.

"Nobody's going to come on my own place and tell me to shut up." His hand started down for his gun.

Sage's gun leaped into his hand with a speed that halted the rancher's move. "I'm doing it, Yake. Now keep your trap shut and think it over. You don't want a range war any more than these homesteaders do. You might get rid of the settlers and probably kill a lot of women and children in the process. You could be proud of that! And you wouldn't have many cattle and probably no home yourself when it was done." He turned on Masterson. "Get going, Abe."

Masterson, still scowling, mounted and wheeled his horse out of the yard.

Sage waited until he was gone, then put his gun in its holster and, turning his back, rode after Masterson.

XIV

Monday brought the crew of homesteaders back to work on the ditch, but there was a tension among the men that hadn't been there before. Sage could read the signs. These men weren't content to let Yake get away without paying for the destruction of Masterson's field of corn. Tempers flared over minor incidents. And the work failed to progress as rapidly as Sage knew it must if he were to win his race against the calendar.

When the sun went down that night, the ditch had plowed its way like a lazy serpent through the prairie grass almost halfway from the dam to the first homestead. But Sage shook his head as he and Hoyt surveyed the work. Only five more days to complete it. Next Sunday would be the first day of October.

"Seen anything of Trenton today?" Sage asked Hoyt as they turned back to the ranch.

"I haven't seen him for nearly a week," Hoyt said. "He knows we're onto him. Slim said he saw him in Stirrup this morning."

Sage nodded. "As long as he's here, we can look for more trouble."

"Think he cut the fence and turned those Circle Y cows into Masterson's corn?"

"I wouldn't be surprised," Sage said slowly. "For some reason, he wants this irrigation ditch stopped. A war would do the job."

"The way these settlers are grumbling, it could start any second."

Sage was thinking about that when the men came to work the next morning. But he forgot it the minute he saw the rider pounding across the prairie from the direction of town. It was Munn, and Sage frowned as he waited for him.

Munn jerked his horse to a halt. "Been a murder in town," he shouted.

Sage grabbed the man's arm. "Who?"

"Ben Trenton," Munn said, his eyes wild with excitement. "Stabbed with a knife."

Sage wheeled to Hoyt. "Keep things going here, Red. I'm going to have a look."

Sage swung into the saddle and put his horse to a

lope toward Stirrup.

In town, he went directly to Doc Merrick's office. Merrick, as coroner, would have what information there was to be had. Sage found the office half full and waited until it was cleared before approaching the little doctor.

"What happened, Doc?" he asked.

Merrick sighed and shrugged. "Somebody jabbed a knife in that lawyer's back."

"When?"

"Last night sometime. Probably about midnight."

Sage nodded. That changed the picture. He had thought from Munn's excited report that it had just happened. "A fight?" he asked.

Merrick shook his head. "He was asleep in the hotel. Must have been a sound sleeper."

A chill ran over Sage. How well he knew Trenton was a sound sleeper.

"Any clues as to who did it?"

"Nothing definite," Merrick said. "That's not my line. I'm just the coroner. I find out what killed them, not who."

"But you do know something," Sage pressed.

"Maybe. Lots of people didn't like Trenton. Some seemed to hate him."

"Who, for instance?"

Merrick frowned. "Persistent, aren't you?"

"He was my lawyer, you know."

"But not your bosom pal." The doctor turned to some papers on his desk.

Sage leaned over the desk. "What do you mean by that?"

Merrick shrugged. "Nothing that you don't already know. There'll be few tears shed over Trenton's passing."

Sage studied Merrick for a minute. "Doc, can you name one person who hated Trenton enough to kill him?"

Merrick looked up from his papers and folded his hands on his desk. "I'm not a good enough student of human nature to know how much a person must hate a man to kill him. But very few people hated Ben Trenton more than Tess Brantley did. Now mind," he added hastily, "I didn't say she killed him. But I do know she hated the ground he walked on."

Sage was silent a moment, considering Merrick's words. He knew, too, that Tess had hated Trenton. But that was all he knew about their relationship.

"Why did she hate him?" he asked.

Merrick shrugged. "I don't know. Maybe they

crossed swords somewhere along the way."

"Any other ideas?"

Merrick shook his head. "None that I'm telling."

Sage went back into the street and paused in front of the drugstore that pressed hard against the doctor's office. How much did Merrick really know? Was he guessing about Tess Brantley? Sage had a sick feeling in the pit of his stomach. Tess was no angel, he knew, but murder was a pretty gruesome thing.

Across the street a man came out of the store that catered to the homesteader trade. Sage frowned a little. Cal Ufford was supposed to be working on the ditch, but here he was in town. And even from a distance, Sage could see that he was excited.

Ufford stood on the porch of the grocery and watched the street to the east. Sage turned his attention that way and saw a little cloud of dust rising in the distance. Two riders were under that dust, kicking it up into the quiet morning air. Booted heels clipped quickly across the porch behind Sage, and Sage turned to see Doc Merrick at his elbow.

"That's probably Sheriff Sullivan from Cottonwood," Merrick said, pointing to the dust.

"You send for him?"

"Sure. Murder's a job for the law."

Sage watched the two riders come into town. One of the men was the sour-faced clerk from the store down the street a couple of doors. Merrick evidently had sent him for the sheriff. Sullivan was a huge man with a full beard reaching down to the star he wore on his leather vest. He swung down in front of the drugstore and heaved himself up on the porch.

"Howdy, Merrick," he said in a voice that matched his size. "Hear there's been a killing."

Merrick, looking like a midget beside Sullivan, nodded vigorously. "A lawyer got a knife in the back last night."

Sage's attention turned to Ufford, who came hurriedly across the street. He had obviously been waiting for the sheriff's arrival. Sullivan's attention turned to the homesteader as soon as Ufford stepped up on the porch.

"I think Mr. Ufford knew Ben Trenton. Maybe he can give you some leads."

Sullivan twisted his huge bulk around. "How about it, fellow?" he rumbled.

"I may be of some help," Ufford said, his eagerness suddenly giving way to reluctance. "I knew Ben Trenton, but I didn't know all his enemies."

"One enemy might be enough," Sullivan said, "providing it's one with a reason for killing him."

Ufford was silent for a minute, then nodded. "I reckon I could name one who had a reason for killing him."

"Who?" Merrick snapped impatiently.

"I ain't saying she did it," Ufford said quickly. "I'm just saying she had a reason."

Sullivan caught Ufford's arm. "Who are you talking about?"

Ufford twisted uncomfortably in the giant's grasp. "Tess Brantley," he said finally in a shrill, unnatural voice.

Sage could see from the look in Merrick's eyes that the noose was tightening around Tess Brantley's neck. "Why did she hate Trenton so much?" he demanded as Sullivan released Ufford.

"I ain't saying any more," Ufford said sullenly. "I wouldn't have said this much, but I feel it's my duty as a citizen of the community to bring a murderer to justice."

"You seemed mighty anxious to do it," Sage said, and spun on his heel.

He got his horse and pounded out of town. He wanted to talk to Tess before Sullivan could reach her.

The TS was as silent as a tomb when Sage rode into

the yard. Turning, he galloped back to the ditch. Hoyt met him a hundred yards from the workers. When Sage told his foreman of the latest developments, Hoyt turned red in the face.

"Tess wouldn't kill anybody," he exploded, jamming a first into his hand. "Trenton needed killing, but Tess didn't do it."

"May be a little hard to convince the sheriff or a jury."

"They don't have any evidence."

Sage nodded. "That's true. But there's no telling what may turn up when they get to poking around. Tess had a secret hate for Trenton."

Hoyt nodded. "I know. But she wouldn't kill him."

"I hope you're right. How's the work going?"

"Not fast enough. They'll finish the gate today. Water is backed up almost to it. There'll be water ready to go in the ditch by Sunday, but the ditch won't be done. How will Trenton's death affect that will?"

Sage shook his head. "It won't change the provisions any. I'm going to see if I can find Tess."

Wheeling his horse, Sage started back down the creek. He'd take a good look around the TS. Maybe Merrick and Ufford were right in suspecting Tess, and she had pulled stakes. If so, he intended to find out.

But before he got to the TS again, he discovered that his guesswork was off. From a little draw north of the ranch, two horsemen were coming. Sage quickly recognized the huge bulk of Sheriff Sullivan, and the other rider was Tess Brantley.

Sullivan and Tess turned down the river toward town and Sage followed at a leisurely pace. Only when they pulled into town did Sage urge his horse forward. He was just a few yards behind them when they dismounted in front of Merrick's office. Sage stopped at the drugstore hitchrack and followed the sheriff and Tess into the doctor's office.

"What did she tell you?" Merrick asked Sullivan as he offered Tess a chair.

"Nothing," Sullivan said, " 'cause I haven't asked her anything yet. There's a time for questions."

Merrick frowned. "Didn't you even tell her why you were bringing her in?"

Tess answered, "He said Ben Trenton had been killed, and he wanted me to come in and help him solve the murder."

Sage leaned against the wall. If Tess was guilty of the murder, she was certainly a cool character.

Merrick jerked a thumb at Sage. "Do you want him here, Sullivan?"

The sheriff shrugged. "He can stay if he wants to. I'm only interested in what she can tell me. Did you know Ben Trenton well, Miss Brantley?"

"Too well," Tess said.

"Did you hate him?"

"I certainly did."

"Careful what you say, Tess," Sage interrupted. "They're trying to pin this on you."

Tess came off her chair, her eyes flashing at Sullivan. "I didn't kill him, if that's what you think.'

"But you did hate him enough to kill him," Sullivan persisted.

"I hated him," Tess said sharply. "But I didn't kill him."

"Why did you hate him?" Merrick asked.

"That's something in the past that has nothing to do with this," Tess said, her lips thin.

"It may have a lot to do with it," Sullivan said, his voice softer than Sage had heard it before.

Tess studied the faces of the sheriff and the doctor. Her chin quivered a little, then set in a hard line. "All right. I'll tell you if it will do you any good. Several years ago Ben Trenton and I were married. I had a child. And when it was too late, I found out that he was a beast. I ran away from him. The baby was a girl, but I had to give her away, because I couldn't give her the kind of home I wanted her to have. I came out here, hoping I'd never see Ben Trenton again. I'm glad he's dead. But I didn't kill him."

Merrick sighed. "I guess you had reason to hate him."

Sullivan nodded. "Reason enough to kill him, too."

Sage pushed away from the wall. "You've got to have evidence to convict a person, Sullivan. What are you going to use to convict Tess?"

The sheriff scratched his head. "Haven't got a thing yet but a motive. But usually the evidence crops up. I've got some leads."

"You can't hold her without evidence," Sage insisted.

Sullivan frowned at Sage. "You keep out of this. It's my job to solve this crime."

Merrick broke in. "Hampton is right, Sheriff. You don't have any grounds for holding her."

"I'll stay in the country," Tess said angrily. "If you find any evidence that I killed Ben Trenton you won't have to hunt for me."

Sullivan glared at Tess, then at Merrick. "What about it, Doc? Can I trust her?"

"She'll be here if she says she will," Merrick said.

Sage rode back to the TS with Tess, then went on to his Flying H. Some of Trenton's things were still there. There might be a clue in them. Tess hadn't killed Trenton, Sage was certain. But she'd never be cleared of suspicion until the guilty one was found.

But one glance at Trenton's room told him he wasn't going to get the first look at the lawyer's things. Trenton's possessions were strung over the room where someone had hurriedly dropped them.

In one corner, Sage found an envelope with no address that had been torn open. The contents were gone. The envelope had been sealed, but there was nothing to give Sage any clue as to what had been in it. Evidently that envelope had been the object of the search, for the upheaval seemed to end right there. There was a little box of papers, and only two or three of them had been taken out.

Carefully Sage started through the other papers. There was one envelope that he recognized as the one Trenton had had in his pocket the day he had read the will in Stirrup. It was a long brown envelope and had: "To be opened only in case the provisions of my will are not met" written on the outside. The end of the envelope was torn off, and Sage decided the burglar had done it while looking for the paper he wanted.

Since the envelope was already open, Sage had no qualms about taking out the papers and reading them. Another piece of the puzzle dropped in place. The paper stated that the Flying H was to go to Ben Trenton or his heirs if Sage Hampton did not meet the provisions set forth in the will.

XV

Wade crossed a slough that backed off from the creek a quarter of a mile above the Circle Y. A meadow lark, balancing on a swaying cattail, serenaded the traveler, but Sage didn't hear. His mind was already ahead, trying to anticipate Yake's reaction to his visit.

But Clem Yake was unpredictable. Before Sage could dismount, Yake came out of the veranda of his big house.

"Just keep your seat till you've stated your business," Yake said curtly.

Sage settled back in his saddle, his eyes quickly scanning the ranch house behind Yake and the yard to his left. Before he could ask a question, Yake continued:

"I suppose you're here to blow your horn again about those cattle that got in Masterson's corn?"

Sage shook his head. "That's done and best forgotten. I'm not here to beat the drums for the homesteaders."

For a moment, Yake eyed his visitor belligerently, then sighed. "All right, Hampton. Get down and say your piece."

As Sage dismounted, a man came out of the door behind Yake and took up a position against the wall.

"Are you determined to have war with the settlers?" Sage asked.

"That's up to them. But if they make one move, they'll get hot lead rammed down their scrawny necks. They don't have any business out there on that plain, anyway."

"You'd like to have an excuse to run them out, wouldn't you?"

"I sure ain't going to dodge any." Yake frowned. "I thought you said you didn't come to talk for them."

"I didn't." For a minute Sage was silent. He studied Yake's seamed face intently when he asked his next question.

"Do any of your men carry knives?"

Yake didn't flinch as he stared at Sage. Then his face began to work, and anger burned up to the roots of his hair. "If you're trying to say me or one of my boys knifed that lawyer, Trenton, you've got more gall than a snake-bit sheepherder. I ain't sorry the mealy-mouthed varmint is dead, but you'll have a hard time proving the Circle Y did it."

"I'm not accusing; I'm just asking," Sage said

quietly.

"Well, go somewhere else and ask. Questions like that ain't welcome here."

Sage nodded and mounted his horse. "I didn't expect them to be. But somebody's a little handy with a knife, and I figure on finding out who it is."

"That's all right by me," Yake snapped. "But don't go snooping around the Circle Y. Some of my boys have mighty itchy fingers."

Sage rode out of the Circle Y yard, satisfied that his plan had worked. There had been rage in Yake's face but not guilt.

Cutting across the prairie toward the homesteads, Sage planned his next visit. Nate Munn had been unusually affected by the murder of Trenton. Maybe it had been an act, played up to give the impression of shock. According to Merrick, Trenton had been killed in his sleep about midnight. Anybody in the valley could have done it and been far from the scene by morning. Surly Nate Munn was a logical suspect.

The road led past Masterson's soddy, and Sage waved to the little girl playing in the late sunlight in the yard. She responded timidly. Sage saw nothing of the girl's mother, and Abe, he supposed, hadn't returned from work on the ditch.

Coming to Ferris' soddy, he reined up in spite of himself. But before he dismounted he saw a man leading a horse around the corner of the soddy and wished he hadn't stopped. He should have known Cal Ufford would be there. Next Sunday was the date set for the wedding, and he supposed there were a lot of plans to be made.

Debbie was with Ufford, and she smiled a greeting at Sage, although Ufford only glared at him. That glare changed to a frown as he led his horse out to the trail.

"Where have you been all day?" he demanded. "You must not be very anxious to get that ditch finished by Sunday."

Sage's face was grim. "It means plenty to me. But there were other things I had to do today."

"What's more important than that ditch?"

"Catching my brother's murderer," Sage said evenly. "And while you're talking about missing work, what were you doing in town this morning?"

Ufford scowled and his face reddened. "I didn't—I mean, I broke a shovel handle and had to go to town for a new one."

"Didn't Red have some extras? He's supposed to keep some."

"He was out," Ufford said, and swung up on his

horse. "You're going to have to tend to business better if you aim to finish that ditch." He spoke softly to Debbie. "I'll be back tonight, Debbie."

Ufford kicked his horse into a lope toward his homestead only a quarter of a mile down the road. Debbie turned to face Sage as he dismounted. Sage met her eyes, and his fingers, still gripping the saddle horn, dug into the leather covering the wooden pommel. How could a man like Cal Ufford claim possession of such a woman as this?

"I suppose you want to see Daddy?" Debbie said.

Sage sighed. "I reckon."

Her face grew sober. "Was Cal in town this morning?"

Sage nodded. "Yes. Guess he couldn't work without a shovel handle."

He knew Ufford had been lying about his reason for being in town and he was sure Debbie knew it, too. He mentally kicked himself for covering up for Ufford.

He was still trying to analyze his own actions when Debbie led him into the house. John Ferris was building a fire in the little cook stove. He turned with a smile of greeting.

"Glad you stopped, Sage. You'll have supper with us, of course?"

Sage shook his head. "No. I've got some things to do before dark. I've been scouting around, trying to pick up the trail of a murderer."

Ferris didn't seem surprised. "I heard about Trenton. Too bad. Murder is a terrible thing. But I doubt if Trenton deserves as much pity as some people might expect."

Sage looked sharply at the old man. Those were the harshest words he had ever heard him speak about anyone. "You didn't think he was such a good man?"

"Obviously he was the one who stole that money from you to keep us from getting our dam and irrigation ditches finished. A man who would do that is a man to be pitied only because he must live with an evil heart. Have you found any trace of the murderer?"

Sage shook his head wearily. "Not yet. But I feel sure that when I do, I'll be on the trail of the man who killed my brother, too."

"Do you suspect anyone?" Debbie asked.

"Suspicions won't hang anybody," Sage answered evasively. "I've got another call to make tonight. I'd better be moving along."

"Will the ditch be done by Sunday?" Ferris asked.

Sage sighed. "I'm afraid it won't be. There isn't enough time."

"Isn't there a chance you'll make it?"

"Of course. If there wasn't, I reckon we'd all quit now."

"Every man on the job counts then, doesn't he?" Debbie asked softly, and Sage knew she was thinking of Ufford's accusation that he was shirking his job.

"I'll be back on the ditch as soon as I catch my man or the trail runs out."

"Couldn't that wait until after Sunday?"

Sage shook his head. "Opportunity doesn't come around begging very often. And there's nothing harder to follow than a cold trail."

"He must do as he sees best," Ferris said gently.

"Of course, Daddy," Debbie agreed. "I didn't mean to criticize. But we need that water so much."

"You'll get it," Sage promised rashly.

He went back to his horse and angrily headed him into the road to the west.

Nate Munn was home, and he came up the steps of his dugout when he heard Sage ride into the yard. Recognizing his visitor, he wheeled to go back down the steps, but Sage stopped him with a sharp command. "Hold it, Munn! You won't need your gun."

Munn, his face drawn into a dark scowl, turned back. "What do you want, Hampton?"

Sage leaned over the saddle horn. Munn was unarmed unless he carried a knife. Sage intended to find out about that. "I want to ask some questions. What did Ben Trenton have to do with you?"

"Nothing," Munn said quickly. "I didn't kill him. You can't pin that on me."

Sage swung off his horse. "I didn't accuse you of killing Trenton. I only asked what business you had with him."

Munn retreated a step. "I didn't have any business with him."

Sage caught the man's shirt front. "That's a lie, Munn. You wouldn't get so excited over the death of a stranger."

"I don't know what you're driving at," Munn said sullenly.

Sage made a quick search of Munn and found no knife. That lessened the chance that he was Trenton's murderer.

"I want to know what deal you had cooked up with Trenton."

"I didn't have any deal with him."

Sage balled his fist under Munn's chin. "You're lying, Munn. You wouldn't get so het up over the murder of your own mother unless you thought you'd lose something by it. You lost out on a pay-off of some kind when Trenton was killed."

Fear crept over Munn's twisted features. "All right," he mumbled. "So you know. But I didn't kill him."

"Do you know who did?"

Munn's teeth showed in a snarl. "If I did, I'd fix him so he wouldn't kill anybody else."

"What did you and Trenton have cooked up?"

"Nothing," Munn said, backing away. "He was paying me, that's all."

"Paying you for what?"

Munn hesitated. "I had to have money," he whined. "I couldn't make a living here."

Sage made a guess. "Trenton was paying you to break up our machinery, wasn't he?"

Munn nodded. "You might as well know one time as another." He stepped forward eagerly. "I wasn't the only one. I can tell you a lot more for a price."

Contempt boiled through Sage. "You won't get any pay from me."

Rage darkened Munn's face as he stepped back to the top of the stairway leading down into his dugout. "Then I won't tell anything. You can whittle me up if you're man enough, but I won't tell."

Sage watched the homesteader for a minute. The

man was a weakling in some ways, but right now, after Sage's rebuff, he would be strong enough to keep any secret he held. Sage spun on his heel and mounted.

"Don't come back to work any more, Munn. If I catch you near the dam or the ditch, I'll give you a ride over the sagebrush on the end of a rope."

Sage wheeled his horse toward the northwest and the Flying H. For a while he couldn't get his mind off Munn. Then he reached the end of the ditch where the workers had quit for the night and reined up.

It was deep twilight, but the light seemed to make the slope down to the homesteads more pronounced. It should be easy work from there down to those farms, Sage thought; easy enough so that it was still possible it could be done by Sunday.

Hoyt was at the ranch, waiting eagerly for Sage's report. His face fell when Sage admitted he had found little that would help solve either Ross' or Trenton's murder. But Hoyt couldn't stay depressed for long. Work had moved along so well today that now it seemed likely the ditch would be done by Sunday.

Supper was barely over when Sage caught the sound of a horse. Hoyt heard it, too, and rose from his chair.

"Better douse that light," Sage suggested, hurrying to the door to peer out as the kerosene lamp behind him flickered once and went out, struck by a puff from Hoyt.

Sage realized his caution was wasted when the rider came on boldly, finally reining up in front of the door. "It's Tess Brantley," he said over his shoulder as he hurried out to the girl. Fear was stamped on her face as she dismounted and looked nervously over her back-trail.

"I'm glad you're home," she said.

"What's the matter?" Sage demanded as Hoyt moved around Sage to take Tess' arm.

"I'm scared, that's all," Tess said, laughing nervously.

"Better come in and calm down a bit."

Tess came as far as the doorway and stopped. "I don't know why I'm acting this way. I never was afraid before."

"Afraid of somebody after what you told today in town?" Sage guessed.

Tess nodded. "Maybe I'm borrowing trouble, but I don't think so."

"Who are you scared of?" Hoyt asked.

Tess shook her head. "I can't tell. I might be wrong; I probably am."

"I wish I knew," Hoyt said savagely, clenching his

fists.

"Would you like to stay here tonight?" Sage offered.

"No," Tess said. "I'll go back home. Marie, my cook, is there. She'll be company."

Sage studied the girl's face. She was afraid. And she hadn't ridden over here just for the exercise. But she was too proud to ask for help. He glanced at Hoyt, who was watching Tess, concern on his freckled face. Sage grinned.

"I could lend you a bodyguard," he said. "I don't think Red would object too much."

"I sure wouldn't," Hoyt said quickly. "You ought to have a man around over there."

Tess smiled in relief. "I would be grateful if you would stay at the ranch. I don't quite trust my two riders. I'm not sure what might happen after the things I told today."

"You won't need Red through the day, will you?"

"I can manage when it's light enough to see," Tess said, confidence back in her voice.

Sage watched Hoyt and Tess Brantley until the darkness swallowed them. Then he turned back to clean up the supper dishes, wondering who Tess was afraid of and why she wouldn't tell. If he knew that, he might be a lot closer to Ross Hampton's murderer.

XVI

On Wednesday, with only four days left for the wedding, Debbie began making the final arrangements. There was so much to do that it almost staggered her to consider it all.

With an efficiency born of determination, she saddled her pony and rode east along the road toward town. Her first stop was at Masterson's. Ruth came to the door as Debbie slid off her horse.

"It's nice to see you, Debbie," Ruth Masterson said, wiping her hands on her apron. "I was telling Abe this morning I wished you'd stop by soon."

Debbie went into the little soddy, warmed as she always was by the welcome she got at the Mastersons'. Today it seem especially good to her, as if she had been chilled and had suddenly come to a warming fire.

"You're coming to the wedding Sunday, aren't

you?"

"We wouldn't miss it for anything," Ruth said enthusiastically. "That will be the most wonderful day in your life."

Debbie nodded, suddenly finding it hard to say anything. She didn't feel as if she were approaching the most wonderful day in her life.

Ruth laid a hand on her arm. "The prospect of such a sudden change in your life probably has you confused," she said gently. "That's nothing to worry about. I doubt if there ever was a bride who didn't have doubts on her wedding day."

Debbie squeezed the work-roughened hand of the homesteader's wife. Ruth was right, of course. Every bride-to-be had doubts. She was no different. She had no reason to question for an instant the decision she had made.

"I came down to see if Ramona would be flower girl at the wedding," she said.

"Of course she will," Ruth said. "You suggested it two weeks ago, and I've been working on her dress. Let me show it to you."

Debbie followed Ruth into the bedroom. The dress was pretty, though not made from fancy cloth, and Debbie could imagine how cute Ramona would look in it. She was admiring the expert needlework in the dress when she glanced up and saw Ruth peering out the back window toward the eastern boundary of their little farm.

"Something wrong, Ruth?" Debbie asked quickly, seeing the worried frown on her friend's face.

Ruth turned away from the window. "I was just looking for Abe."

"Isn't he working on the ditch today?"

"He hasn't worked there since Monday. He's trying to keep the Circle Y cattle out of our field."

"Have they been back again?"

Ruth nodded. "Twice. Abe thinks Clem Yake and his men drive the cattle over this way and hope they'll get into our corn. Abe swears he'll kill those cows if they get in the corn again." She sank on the bed. "You know what that will mean."

"You've got to stop him, Ruth. Clem Yake is just waiting for an excuse to start a war."

"I know. But men have their pride. Abe is no different from the others; he won't tolerate being run over. He'd rather die fighting."

"But doesn't he think about you and Ramona?"

Ruth laid a hand on Debbie's arm. "He is thinking about us. At least his pride makes him believe he is doing it all for us."

"But what if he's killed?"

"A man's pride won't consider that possibility. Abe is proud, but I wouldn't have him any other way."

Debbie rose to go, and Ruth followed her to the door. "If you need any help getting ready for Sunday, just let me know. Enjoy every minute of it, Debbie. It's the best time of your life."

Debbie rode back to the road and pointed her horse toward the creek. Her next stop was to be the TS, and in spite of Tess's friendliness at the church dedication, Debbie had her misgivings as she reined across the creek and into the ranch yard.

The place was as silent as a tomb when Debbie stopped her horse at the hitchrack, and she wondered if the ranch was deserted. Then the door opened and Tess came out on the porch. Her face was pale beneath the tan, and Debbie knew she was facing someone more afraid, for some reason, than she was. Behind Tess, Debbie caught a glimpse of a man she recognized as Red Hoyt. She wondered about that but turned her attention to Tess as the TS owner welcomed her.

"Get down and come in, Debbie," Tess said, and Debbie marveled at the warmth in her voice.

Debbie dismounted and climbed the steps to the little

porch.

"I stopped by to see about that lace you offered to loan me," Debbie said, suddenly embarrassed at the thought of borrowing from Tess Brantley.

"Of course," Tess said quickly. "Come on in. I'll get it. But I didn't mean to lend it to you. I'm giving it to you. And I hope it brings you better luck than it did me."

"Did you have it on your wedding dress?"

Tess laughed harshly. "I did."

Tess went for the lace, and Debbie looked around for Hoyt. He was in the partition doorway, trying not to notice what Tess and Debbie were saying. Debbie saw the heavy gun he wore and wondered about that. Why was he there? And why the gun?

Glancing through a back window, she saw Hoyt's horse. Apparently he had just come from work on the ditch. Maybe it was Hoyt who was frightening Tess.

Tess brought the lace and handed it to Debbie, and Debbie said impulsively, "You'll come to the wedding, won't you?"

"If you really want me to."

"I do," Debbie said, fingering the lace.

Tess smiled. "Then I'll be there."

Debbie started toward the door but stopped when

Hoyt stepped forward.

"Don't happen to be riding toward the ditch, do you?" he asked.

Debbie turned. "I thought I would."

"Mind if I ride along?"

Tess followed them to the porch. "You'll be back tonight, Red?"

"I'll come straight from work," he promised.

Debbie thanked Tess for the lace and rode out of the yard and across the creek with Hoyt.

She was surprised at the progress of the ditch. Hoyt went directly to his job, and Debbie swung around to the spot where Sage was working with a crew of shovelers. He stopped work and came over to her horse.

"Looks like you might make it," Debbie said.

He grinned. "We're going to try, if we can just keep the men working."

"Why did you send Hoyt down to the TS when you need men so bad?"

Sage grinned broadly. "I didn't send him. He thought something was wrong down there. He's pretty worried about Tess' well-being."

Debbie caught his meaning and dropped the subject. She looked at Sage and wished she could say something that would tell him how much she appreciated the effort he was making to get water to the homesteaders.

"You'll come to the wedding next Sunday, won't you? It's at two o'clock."

He hesitated and his face flushed. "Well, I may be busy. I don't know—"

With a shock, she realized her mistake. He had let her know how he felt about her the afternoon after the church dedication. Of course he wouldn't want to come to her wedding. How big a blunder could she make! She knew her face was burning with embarrassment when he looked up.

"I'm sorry, Sage," she mumbled.

He reached up impulsively and caught her hand. "I'll be there, Debbie. And good luck."

She kicked her horse into a lope toward home. Why had she made such a fool of herself? And Sage, when he had seen her embarrassment, had agreed to come to her wedding to make her feel better. But why should he care how she felt?

She sewed the lace on her dress during the afternoon and hid the dress from Cal that night when he came over. He was in a dark mood, and she doubted if he would have noticed it even if she had been wearing it.

"What's the matter, Cal?" she asked after he had sat for ten minutes scowling silently into space.

He roused himself with a sigh. "Everything. Yake's going to start a war. Hampton isn't going to get the ditch done, and I don't think he cares much."

"He seemed to be working hard at it today."

"That's another thing, Debbie. You shouldn't be hanging around Hampton. What will people say?"

Surprise stunned Debbie. "I haven't been hanging around Sage, Cal. Today was the first I'd seen him since Sunday at the dedication. And he was working. It looked to me like he'd get the job done."

The scowl deepened on Ufford's face and he said nothing. He was jealous, Debbie thought, but she felt no shame or guilt. She had given him no reason to doubt her.

Ufford's stay was short, and Debbie wasn't sorry to see him go. Not too often had he shown her the mood he was flaunting tonight, and she didn't care to prolong the visit. Tomorrow he would be himself again.

She was tired and went to bed early. She had barely gotten into bed when she heard a horse pull up outside; then her father answered a knock on the door. She waited but didn't hear anyone come in. Then John Ferris opened the door to her room and poked his head inside.

"I've got a little job to do tonight, Debbie. I won't

be gone long. Don't worry about me."

She sat up in bed. "Where are you going?"

"Not far," he said evasively. "Don't worry."

He withdrew quickly, leaving Debbie frowning thoughtfully. It wasn't like her father to go off, especially at night, and not tell her where he was going.

Debbie heard him return about midnight. But even the next morning, he would tell her nothing about his nocturnal business. He only smiled at her questions.

"I promised not to tell," he said. "You'll find out when the time comes. It's nothing for you to lose any sleep about."

Debbie dismissed it from her mind.

XVII

The dam was finished, the gates were in place, but the ditch to the homesteads was not done. And tomorrow was the first day of October.

Sage stood on the bluff overlooking the dam and watched the few homesteaders who had come to work that day head for their homes. Hoyt, standing beside Sage, heaved a weary sigh. Sage knew what was on his mind.

"I wonder what will happen to all this when the new owners, whoever they are, take over," Sage said thoughtfully.

"Hard to say," Hoyt said, shaking his head. "We gave it a good try. If the settlers had stayed with us this week, we'd have made it."

"I'd like to wring Yake's neck," Hoyt growled. "You can't tell me he wasn't kicking up this threat of trouble just to keep these men guarding their homes and not working on the ditch."

Sage turned back toward the Flying H barn and corral. "It doesn't make much difference why he did it. It's done, and the ditch isn't. That's that."

"If Ross could have his say now, you'd get this place and stay here to finish that irrigation ditch, too," Hoyt said, pounding a fist into his palm. "It's too bad men can't make their will six months after they die, instead of before." He picked up the reins of his horse. "Got to be heading home—I mean, down to stand guard for Tess."

Sage shook off his gloom and grinned at his foreman. "Couldn't be you're working up a new job for yourself?"

Hoyt swung into his saddle. "Can't tell. I might be that lucky."

Sage watched Hoyt ride down the valley toward the TS, wondering at Hoyt's buoyancy every time he talked about getting back to the TS. Apparently he was getting along pretty well with Tess Brantley. Maybe he could get a job on the TS when the new owners took over the Flying H.

Sage's plans extended only through Monday. Tomorrow, Sunday, he would go to Debbie's wedding as he had promised. Then Monday he would ride to Cottonwood, find a good lawyer and turn over the envelope of instructions that were to be followed if Sage failed to get the water to the homesteads on the date set. After that, he would be free to ride on. The lawyer could find Ben Trenton's relatives and turn the Flying H over to them.

But Monday worried Sage very little. Sunday was the day he dreaded.

He cooked supper, but it was tasteless, and he threw most of it out. After he blew out the light he sat for a long time staring through the window at the road leading down to the dam, dimly lit by a slice of a moon hanging in the western sky.

His thoughts were wandering aimlessly miles away when a figure on the road pierced his thoughts like a pin in a bubble. He sat motionless for a minute, watching the figure move slowly up toward the house. At first he thought it was an animal of some kind; then he realized it was a man, crawling flat on his stomach.

Sage moved quickly toward his gun belt, hanging over a nail behind the door. He was glad he had decided to sit in the dark tonight. He held his gun ready as he stood to one side of the window and watched the man crawl closer.

His gun began to sag in his hand as he watched. Then he jammed it into his waistband and turned to the door. The man wasn't trying to sneak in on him; he was hurt, and apparently hurt pretty bad.

Still Sage had his hand on the gun when he opened the door. He had been fooled before. The man stopped crawling when he heard the door open and turned a pain-twisted face up to Sage. Sage moved forward and knelt beside him.

"What happened, Munn?" he asked.

The usually surly face of the homesteader was drawn with pain. "I fell off my horse—back at the dam," he said, his words coming hard.

"Before that," Sage insisted.

"I—I got caught—"

Munn's head dropped and Sage reached for his wrist. The pulse was still there, but weak. Lifting the man like a baby, Sage carried him inside and laid him on the bed. Then he lit the lamp and examined him. There was a knife wound high in his chest.

For the next half-hour, Sage was so busy heating water and dressing the wound that he lost track of his own worries. When the work was done, Munn roused from unconsciousness.

"Better take it easy," Sage said. "I'll get Doc Merrick."

Munn reached out a hand and caught Sage's arm, shaking his head weakly. But he didn't try to speak, keeping his eyes closed and breathing hard.

Munn opened his eyes again, and this time he made signs that he wanted to talk. Sage propped a pillow under his head. But when Munn tried to talk his words were only a jumble and soon faded to a whisper. Then he lapsed into unconsciousness again.

Sage knew he had to have a doctor, and the urgency that pressed him as he saddled his horse was built up by more than just solicitude for the health of Nate Munn. Munn must have something he wanted to tell Sage. Sage could think of no other reason the man would have ridden all the way to the Flying H, wounded as he was.

Doc Merrick was already in bed when Sage knocked on his door, but he was ready to ride in ten minutes and went back to the ranch with Sage. Sage gave him all the information he had about Munn as they rode. Munn was still unconscious when Merrick set to work on him.

"Not so good," the doctor mumbled to himself as he examined the wound. "Could be worse, though."

For half an hour he worked, and the patient roused

twice, only to sink back into oblivion. When he finished, the doctor sighed and snapped his bag shut.

"He'll probably pull through, but he mustn't be moved. How about taking care of him?"

Sage shrugged. "According to the will my brother left, tomorrow's my last day here. I'll take of him tonight, though."

Merrick nodded. "I'll send out somebody tomorrow morning." He stood for a moment looking down at the unconscious homesteader. "Somebody around here is mighty handy with a knife."

"That's what I've been thinking," Sage said. "One reason I want to keep him alive. He can probably tell us a lot of things."

"That's about the only good reason I can think of," Merrick said, and went outside to his horse.

Sage tried to sleep, but Munn stirred restlessly and mumbled incessantly. Finally he was quiet, and Sage slept. He roused when he heard Munn again.

"Hampton."

The word was weak, but there was no trace of the delirium that had marked his jabbering before. Sage got up and leaned over the wounded man.

"Something you want, Munn?"

"I want to talk," Munn said. His eyes were bright,

and Sage touched his forehead and found it hot with fever. But his mind seemed to be clear.

"I'm listening," Sage said.

"Ufford stabbed me," Munn whispered. "Thought he killed me."

"Ufford!" Sage exclaimed.

"Yeah. He killed Trenton, too. I was snooping. Found out. He caught me."

Sage bent lower over Munn as his voice grew weaker. "Why did he kill Trenton?"

"They were partners. Aimed to get this ranch, starve out the settlers, then set up their own kingdom. Trenton double-crossed Ufford."

Munn was getting weaker and a cloud was sifting over his eyes. But Sage had one more question he wanted answered before Munn drifted back into unconsciousness.

"Did Ufford kill Ross?"

"Think so," Munn said, putting a hand to his head. "I can't settle with Ufford. You can. Got a reason."

Munn's eyes closed, and his words became an incoherent mumble again. But there was no sleep left in Sage now. He dropped in the chair by the window and stared out at the place where the dam lay hidden.

XVIII

Sage fretted through the early hours after the sun came up, waiting for the nurse Merrick had promised to send out to care for Munn. The homesteader was still out of his head most of the time, and his fever seemed to be worse. But Sage spent little time worrying about Munn. He had work to do and decisions to make, and he couldn't do either until he could leave the ranch.

A woman drove a light buggy into the yard about nine o'clock. Sage hurried out to put the team in the barn and turn over his nursing duties to her. He had seen the woman once in a store in Stirrup, but he didn't know her. He saw instantly that she was bursting with news.

"I wanted to go to the wedding today," she said as she climbed out of the buggy. "But I figure this is the only safe place in the valley."

"What do you mean?"

"So you haven't heard?" she said, satisfaction in her voice. "Abe Masterson shot a Circle Y critter last evening in his cornfield. Everybody figures there'll be bullets flying before the sun goes down tonight."

Sage was jarred by the impact of the news. The fight that was almost certain to come, coupled with his failure to get water to the farms, would be enough to run the homesteaders out. Maybe Ufford had figured out a way to capitalize on this. But what about the Mastersons? He had liked them, especially little Ramona. They would be the first to feel the force of Clem Yake's wrath.

"You'll find Munn inside," Sage directed the woman. "Use whatever you need that you can find."

He hurriedly put the team away and got out his own horse. Today wasn't going to run along the serene course he had anticipated.

He rode first to Masterson's. Abe Masterson, grim-faced, met him in front of his dugout, a rifle in his hand and a belt gun strapped around his middle.

"Looking for trouble, Abe?"

The homesteader nodded without smiling. "It had to come. A man can't live here and let a range hog's cows eat everything he raises."

"I reckon not," Sage said. "Where are Ruth and Ramona?"

"Ruth took Ramona to church. Ramona will stay. She has to be flower girl at the wedding this afternoon. Ruth is coming back as soon as she can."

"Shouldn't you make her stay at the church? It would be safer."

"I know it would. But she's got a mind of her own. She won't leave me here alone."

"Any help coming from the settlement?"

"Maybe. I don't know. I haven't asked for any. I figure this is my fight."

"You didn't start this fight, Abe. Whoever butchered that beef last summer did that."

"Ufford and Munn did the butchering," Masterson said, seeming to feel free to talk now that guns were going to roll anyway. "But it was like Cal said. The ranchers owed us something for the damage their cattle were doing to our fields, and that was the only way we'd ever get paid."

"This isn't just your fight, Abe. When you're out of the way, the rest of the settlement will be next. Yake wants you all out of here."

"He'll have to put us out," Masterson said grimly, taking a look to the northeast where the Circle Y nestled across the creek.

"Think I'll ride over that way and see what's brewing," Sage said.

"You on friendly terms with Yake?"

Sage grinned. "Hardly. The last time I was there, I

got orders not to come back. But I figure I'll go, anyway."

Sage went around Masterson's field, then cut across the prairie toward the Circle Y. When he dropped down over the last hill above the creek, he could see the activity in the yard of the big ranch. And he saw something else that caused him to swerve his course sharply to the left. A rider was leaving the ranch, heading upstream toward Stirrup. When he saw Sage, he bent low over his saddle and kicked his horse into a run. But Sage was sure he had recognized that tall awkward rider on the big plow horse. It looked like Cal Ufford.

If it was Ufford, he managed to get more speed out of the big-footed horse than Sage would have thought possible. By the time Sage got across the creek, the rider had disappeared completely. Sage spent half an hour trying to locate him, riding as far as town, but finally had to give it up.

Turning back down the creek, he paused on a knoll overlooking the crowded Circle Y yard. There was no need to go in. He would learn nothing more than he could see from there.

A dozen saddled horses were tied at the hitchrack and the corral. Rifle butts protruded from saddle boots.

Men lounged around, guns hanging low from their hips. It was an army ready to move, but waiting for something.

A couple of men went out to their horses and loosened the cinches. Sage frowned. Men once ready to ride were now settling down to wait. He wondered, rubbing his chin thoughtfully. It was possible, he thought, that the rider he had seen leave the ranch had brought some word that had caused them to hold up.

He reined away from the ranch, having satisfied himself that the expected raid on the homesteads was not to take place for a while yet. Perhaps Yake was waiting until the homesteaders all went to the church for the wedding. That struck him as the answer. The homesteaders would be looking for a reprisal this morning, but this afternoon, during the wedding, their vigilance would begin to relax.

He reported his observations to Masterson and a couple of other homesteaders who were with him now, then went on to Cal Ufford's dugout. Keeping his hand on his gun, he scanned the place. But there was no sign of anyone. Ufford apparently was gone. Maybe he was at church; maybe he was out on a questionable mission, such as a trip to the Circle Y.

Dismounting, Sage led his horse around behind the

low sod barn, then went back and down the steps of the dugout. There he had his first surprise. The door was locked. Sage had never found a locked door anywhere in the country before. It raised his suspicions. He wasn't thoroughly convinced yet that Munn had told the truth about Ufford. And though he was inclined to believe Munn, he had to have proof.

Sage slammed his shoulder against the door, and it creaked but held. Going back up the steps, he checked the countryside and found it empty. Then he went back down the steps and threw himself against the door. Wood splintered as the lock ripped from its fastening and the door flew open, banging against the washstand behind it.

Sage began a hurried search. It was after noon now. Ufford was liable to show up at any minute. There was very little in the room that wasn't necessary to simple living—a little stove, a crude table, a couple of chairs and a bed. In one corner was a cupboard that evidently served as a pantry, and in another corner clothes hung from a board full of nails. It was toward this corner that Sage hurried.

A quick glance through the clothes revealed nothing. Then his hand struck something hard. Hanging inside a coat was a long-bladed knife in a heavy sheath. So far Munn's story seemed to be holding up. This was the first knife Sage had seen in the valley that could have struck the fatal blow to Trenton, or slashed cleanly through the rope that had been found around Ross. Probably it was the knife that had ripped into Munn. He slipped the knife, sheath and all, inside his shirt. But still it wasn't proof that Ufford had killed Ross.

Sage looked through the clothes again, then turned to a pile of things beside the stove. A shovel and a pick were there, and a couple of picket pins. And there was a rope. Sage examined it. One end was tied into a crude slip knot. The end of the rope protruding from the knot caught Sage's eye. It had been cut clean, and the rope apparently hadn't been used much since. The ends of the strands weren't even beginning to ravel.

For a long time Sage fingered the rope, making certain. When he threw it down, he was convinced that at last he had located Ross' killer.

He went back and got his horse. There was still no one in sight. Apparently Ufford had dressed for his wedding that morning. Sage couldn't remember seeing a suit hanging among the clothes in the corner. His next move was still uncertain as he rode past Ferris' soddy. It was quiet there. The dugouts beyond showed no sign of life. Apparently everyone was either at the wedding or with Masterson, waiting for Yake to strike.

When he came in sight of the church, he realized that most of the community was there. All the hitch-rack space was used up, and some of the rigs and saddle horses were tied to the back wheels of other rigs.

Sage dismounted outside the circle of buggies and horses. A glance at his watch showed that it was nearly two o'clock. From the looks of the yard, Sage decided that most of the people had come for church and stayed for a picnic dinner. It was an excuse few of the fun-starved homesteaders would pass up.

Inside, he could hear the quiet strains of the organ playing a melody he had never heard before. A murmur of voices drifted out through an open window, and a few men still stood just outside the door.

Sage started forward, then stopped again. He was wearing his old clothes, and the gun swinging from his hip made him look like a savage compared with the men in front of the church who were dressed in their best.

But he hesitated only a moment. Maybe he did look like a savage; maybe he'd act like one when he got in the church. Certainly some people were going to think so. But he had no choice. He didn't like the idea of exposing Ufford in front of Debbie. But he'd be a worse coward to let her marry him, thinking he was something he never had been and never would be.

The men in front of the church stopped talking to stare at Sage as he crowded between them. As he stepped through the doorway, the organ broke into the wedding march. Sage halted just inside the door to size up the situation. Ufford, with another settler as best man, was already in the center of the aisle at the front of the church. Little Ramona Masterson was moving slowly up the aisle, carrying a huge bouquet of flowers, most of them native wild flowers. Just starting up the aisle from the back of the church were Debbie and her father.

The church was packed with people, and every eye was turned on Debbie and John Ferris. Sage was thankful no one had noticed his entrance. Like the others, his eyes focused on Debbie and refused to move. It seemed to Sage that her dress, though homemade, was the prettiest thing he had ever seen, and the lace that trimmed it put a final touch to an already perfect creation.

But Sage knew it wasn't the dress that was dazzling him. It was the girl wearing it. Since the first day he had seen Debbie, she had had the power to sway him as the wind sways a blackbird on a cattail in the marsh.

Today that power was greater than ever.

He tried to look at her face to see if there was a happy smile there. But she was moving up the aisle away from him, and he could get only a glimpse of her profile. And he saw no smile.

Debbie and her father reached the front of the church, and John Ferris stepped forward, turning to face his daughter and Ufford. The music stopped. And Sage knew he had waited as long as he could.

He moved a few steps up the aisle, and Ferris, opening his Bible, paused as he saw Sage for the first time.

"Sorry to bust in like this," Sage said, and every eye in the church darted toward him. He heard a dozen shocked gasps as he spoke again. "I've got something I have to say."

John Ferris put on his sternest frown and glared at Sage. "This is a very solemn thing you're interrupting, Mr. Hampton," he said severely. "Won't you please wait until after the ceremony?"

"I'm afraid not, John." Sage allowed himself only one short look at the horror-stricken face of Debbie.

Ferris controlled his shock in masterful fashion. "All right," he said through tight lips. "Speak and let us hold this interruption to a minimum."

Sage glanced quickly over the room, then brought

his eyes to rest on Ufford. Ufford had gone pale under his tan, and Sage tensed. The lanky homesteader was already suspicious.

"What I have to say may interrupt this ceremony for a long time," Sage said tightly. "I'm accusing Cal Ufford of murdering Ben Trenton and my brother, Ross Hampton."

Men gasped and women screamed. Sage watched Ufford. Out of the corner of his eye, he saw Debbie turn pale and wondered if she would faint. Ufford was the first to recover from his surprise, and Sage guessed it was because he was the least surprised.

"It's a lie," he shouted hoarsely. "He has his own reasons for accusing me and picking this exact time to do it. Is there anyone here who believes I would murder anyone?"

There wasn't. Sage had expected just such a reaction and was prepared for it.

He lifted his left hand for silence. "I know what I'm saying." He reached inside his shirt and brought out the knife. "This is Ufford's knife, the one that killed Ben Trenton."

Relief swept across Ufford's face. "Is that what he intends to use for proof?" he shouted. "That isn't my knife. It may be his own. Maybe he killed Trenton himself."

Sage had convinced no one. Anger was rising swiftly among the men around him. But he still had his bombshell, and now he dropped it.

"Has anyone seen Nate Munn today?"

Sage was watching Ufford while a buzz of excited voices hummed around him. Ufford had suddenly gone white, and his fists clenched at his sides.

"I'll tell you about him," Sage said in the hush that fell before his lifted hand. "He crawled into my place last night more dead than alive. He had been stabbed. He said Ufford tried to kill him because he had found out about the scheme Ufford and Trenton had cooked up to swindle you folks out of every bit of your land. When Trenton double-crossed Ufford, your very pious neighbor here killed him."

"That's a lie!" Ufford screamed.

But there weren't as many heads nodding in agreement with Ufford this time.

"Where is Munn now?" somebody asked.

"At the Flying H, alive and ready to tell what he knows about Ufford."

That statement broke Ufford's restraint. With uncanny speed, the lanky homesteader whipped out a small knife from inside his coat and, with his other hand, caught the little flower girl, Ramona, and jerked her back against him.

"All right, everybody, stand back," he snapped.

No longer was there any resemblance to the pious man who had been a pillar of the church. Ufford was a killer now, a snarling, fear-crazed killer. As men stood too stunned to move, Ufford jabbed the point of his knife against the girl's back.

"Clear the way and don't try to stop me if you want this girl to live!" he muttered. "Hampton, take off your gun."

Sage unbuckled his gun belt and let it fall. "Better give him room," he said. "He'll kill Ramona if you don't."

"I'm not fooling," Ufford snapped.

He moved down the aisle and turned near the door, keeping the girl between him and the crowd. Sage thought of the men who had been outside, hoping they'd take a hand as Ufford stepped through the door. But he saw those men were inside now, apparently attracted by the commotion he had created. Sage knew there wasn't a weapon in the house except his gun and Ufford's knife. The settlers didn't carry guns into a church.

At the door, Ufford paused. "Don't try to follow

me," he ordered. "I'm taking this girl along to make sure you don't."

Tears began streaming down Ramona's face as she recovered from the first shock of what was happening to her. Cries of anguish came from the women, and some pleaded with Ufford to let the little girl go. But he only curled his lip, showing his teeth like a mad dog, and backed through the door.

One woman's cry was louder than the others as she fought her way through the crowd to the door. She would have charged outside if Sage hadn't caught her arm and held her in a tight grip. Only after he had stopped her did he recognize Tess Brantley. Red Hoyt was pushing his way through the crowd to catch Tess' other arm.

"My baby!" Tess cried. "That's my baby!"

"He'll kill her if you go out there, Tess," Hoyt said sharply.

After a minute, she quit struggling and leaned on Hoyt's shoulder, sobbing wildly.

"What did she mean?" Sage asked.

"Just what she said," Hoyt replied. "She gave Ramona to the Mastersons to raise because she couldn't take care of her and run a ranch at the same time."

"Let's do something," a man behind Sage shouted,

pushing toward the door.

"Easy," Sage cautioned. "Watch which way he goes. But don't go out there. He'll carry out his threat."

"He's taking his time about leaving," another man said.

"He knows he's safe now," Sage said. "I'm the only one here with a gun, and I don't dare shoot. I might hit Ramona."

Ferris, shaken but apparently calm again, touched Hoyt's shoulder. "Better take your wife back to a chair."

Sage's head snapped around. "Wife?"

Hoyt grinned in spite of the tension gripping him. "Sure. Ferris married us the other night. I called him out after supper to do it."

"I'll be all right now," Tess said, raising her head and clenching her teeth against the sobs. "If I get the chance, I'll kill Cal Ufford myself."

"We must turn him over to the law to be justly punished," Ferris said gently.

"After all he's done, the law could never punish him enough to satisfy me," Tess said bitterly.

"Has he bothered you before?" Sage asked, buckling his gun around his waist.

"He knew about my marriage to Trenton. I've got

an aristocratic family back in Ohio. I've never told them what happened. Ufford has been blackmailing me, knowing I'd give anything to keep them from finding out."

"He's piling up little boards and shavings," a man reported from a side window. "What do you suppose he's up to?"

Sage moved closer to the door in order to see Ufford better. He was gathering shavings and little scraps of boards left from the building of the church. But always he kept Ramona between him and the building.

Debbie came down from the front of the church to stand beside her father and Sage. Sage looked at her, marveling at the tilt of her chin and her dry eyes. Shock and pain were in her eyes, but no panic or despair. Pride swelled up inside him, as though her show of courage were a personal victory for him.

"I'm sorry, Debbie," he said softly.

"I'm sorry, too, that he's the kind of man he is," she said, her voice barely a whisper.

"He's starting a fire," a man shouted.

Sage looked out and saw smoke rising straight up in the still afternoon air. Ufford piled on more shavings and trash and the smoke thickened.

"It's the signal!" Sage said suddenly.

XIX

"What kind of a signal?" Hoyt demanded, gripping Sage's arm.

"A signal to Yake to tell him that everybody is gone from the homesteads. Yake was ready to ride with his men this morning, but he was waiting for something. And I'm sure I saw Ufford ride away from the Circle Y."

"We've got to get down there and help Abe," a man shouted.

Sage held up his hand. "Not yet. Ufford is still out there. And we want to keep Ramona alive."

"I'll stop Yake," Tess said sharply.

"I thought you wanted these settlers gone from here."

"A woman can change her mind," Tess said. "Anyway, I've made a lot of friends here that I don't intend to lose as neighbors."

"How are you going to stop Yake?" Sage demanded. "He wants this war."

"Yake's greedy but not an unreasonable man. I've handled him before. I can do it again. And I can do better alone."

Sage nodded. "Probably so. When Ufford strikes out, we'll keep on his trail. And don't worry, Tess. We'll get Ramona back safe."

"He's leaving," the man by the window reported. "Took the fastest horse and is holding Ramona in the saddle in front of him, heading north."

The building emptied in a few seconds. Hoyt helped Tess mount a good horse and started her toward the east. Sage got his own horse and mounted. Those with horses were mounted and those in carts and buggies were in their rigs, looking at him. Suddenly he had become their leader.

"We don't dare crowd him too close," Sage said. "Red and I will go ahead and keep him in sight. The rest of you can come or go home."

He and Hoyt started out across the prairie toward the north. Some of the rigs and most of the horsemen followed. Others turned back to their homes to face the threat of Yake's invasion.

Ufford wasn't traveling fast, mainly because he was such an awkward rider that his horse couldn't get into full stride. Sage and Hoyt had little trouble keeping him in sight. Ufford held a steady course, veering to the northwest only when he came to the irrigation ditch.

"Must figure on crossing the dam," Hoyt shouted above the pounding of hooves.

Sage nodded but said nothing. On the other side of the creek, the land was level for the most part. Evidently Ufford felt safer on flat land where there was no chance of being ambushed. While he held Ramona, he wouldn't be pressed unless someone could surprise him.

As they approached the dam, it became evident that Sage had guessed Ufford's strategy. Then, just a few yards from the dam, Ufford turned to look back, jerking the reins and pulling his horse over into the freshly stirred ground at the edge of the ditch. The horse stumbled and went down.

Hoyt gasped, and Sage rose in his stirrups. Ufford's horse struggled to its feet and raced away as Ufford bounded up, made a desperate lunge for the reins and missed. Ramona, apparently unhurt, turned to run, but Ufford, seeing he couldn't get the horse, wheeled and overtook Ramona before Sage could get close enough to take a hand.

"Keep back," Ufford shouted, "or I'll kill her."

"Now what?" Hoyt asked, pulling his horse beside Sage.

"We'll see what he does."

Other riders came up, and soon the rigs stopped behind them. Ufford hadn't moved from the edge of the ditch. He was still holding Ramona as a shield, apparently at a loss to know what he should do next.

"Anything we can do?" Debbie asked, running up from the rig she and her father had driven.

"Maybe." Sage turned to the waiting men. "Fan out in a semicircle from the ditch to the dam. Any guns in the crowd.?"

"Some of us have guns in our buggies," one man said.

"He'll kill the girl," a woman squealed hysterically.

"I don't think so," Sage said. "She's his only hope of getting out of here. If he didn't have Ramona, we'd get him in a minute, and he knows it."

"After we fan out, then what?" Hoyt asked.

"Keep his attention over here. I'll try to sneak up the ditch behind him."

"Can't he cross the ditch?" John Ferris asked.

"He can, but I don't think he will. He's afoot now, and he won't risk making a run for it unless he gets some way to ride."

The rigs and men fanned out, with Sage going to the south end of the line which touched the ditch. Ufford might move down to the crowd and demand a horse or a rig, using Ramona for protection. But Sage didn't believe Ufford had that much nerve. Ufford could see guns in the crowd now, and if he got in the center of the line, somebody might take a shot at him.

Sage dropped over the lip of the ditch and checked to make sure Ufford hadn't seen him, then began moving quietly up the ditch. Ufford was only a few feet from the gate that was holding the water back from the ditch, and Sage marked a spot where he could rise up and get the drop on Ufford.

Over the bank of the ditch, which was four feet high here close to the dam, Sage could hear men calling remarks to Ufford; above, on the bank, he heard Ufford shuffle around. Indecision was driving the man to the breaking point, Sage guessed. Sage got his gun in his hand and had just reached the spot he had picked to rise up behind Ufford's position when he heard a startled oath a few feet ahead of him.

Glancing up, he saw Ufford, who had apparently

decided to cross the ditch, standing on the gate. Sage threw himself sideways as Ufford's knife flashed past him, sinking almost out of sight in the soft dirt. Sage landed against the opposite bank on his shoulder and pushed himself away hurriedly, expecting to see Ufford come sailing down on him. He had dropped his gun as he lunged out of line with the knife, and he couldn't see it in the soft dirt.

But Ufford was still on the gate when Sage looked up. Too late Sage saw the water rushing at him as Ufford threw open the gate. Lunging to the bank, he tried to scramble out of the ditch. But the water caught him, pulling him into its grasp.

Above the roar of the water he heard a terrified scream and, as he caught his feet momentarily on the bottom of the ditch, he saw both Ufford and Ramona splash into the water.

The force of the water was more than Sage could fight. He tried desperately to keep his feet under him and to get to Ramona. But he was washed along on the wild current. Ramona's resistance to the force of the water was less than Sage's, and she came tumbling through the swirling water close to him. He caught her dress as she whirled past.

Then he reached the first curve in the ditch, and the

force of his progress slammed him against the bank. He turned his back to the bank and dug in his heels. He was there, holding Ramona, when Hoyt reached him and dragged him up the bank.

Ramona had taken some water into her lungs and was thoroughly frightened, but some quick work by Debbie revived her. Sage was tired and battered but nothing more.

"What about Ufford?" he asked after he had rested awhile, stretched out in the warm sun.

Ferris, coming along the bank of the ditch from the direction of the homesteads, heard Sage's question.

"Cal is dead," he said. "Drowned."

Ferris turned toward his rig, a tired, bewildered man, his faith battered but still holding firm. Sage stared down into the ditch which had taken Ufford's life.

"Too bad," he said almost to himself. "He didn't get the punishment he deserved."

Debbie, her face white from the shock of the last hour, spoke at Sage's side. "All you wanted was revenge for the death of your brother, wasn't it, Sage?"

Sage sighed. "Maybe so."

" 'Vengeance is mine, saith the Lord,' " she quoted.

"When you stop to think about it," Hoyt said

solemnly, "can you think of any worse punishment for Ufford than to drown? I never saw a man so afraid of water."

"If he hadn't gotten panicky, he probably wouldn't have drowned," Sage said.

A man came along the bank of the ditch, running hard and waving his arms frantically. Sage turned with Hoyt to meet him.

"Shut off the water," he shouted. "It's flooding Munn's dugout."

Sage leaped up on the gate and shut it down, holding the water back in the dam. When he jumped back to the bank of the ditch, Ferris had come back from his little road cart, new hope shining in his face.

"Do you realize what this means?" he said excitedly. "This is the first of October, and you've got the water to the homesteads."

"But the ditch isn't done," Hoyt said, a puzzled frown on his fact.

"The will didn't say anything about a ditch, did it? It merely said the dam must be completed and water running to the homesteads. That is done."

Sage felt as if somebody had lifted a great weight off his shoulders. Only during the last few days had he realized how much the Flying H had come to mean to him. He glanced at Debbie. There was another reason he had come to like this valley. Hope, almost dead, was springing to life again. And after time had healed some wounds, he'd find out what chance hope had of surviving.

Hoyt suddenly pointed to the southeast. "Tess is coming. Looks like the others are with her."

Tess came up ahead of the others and ran to Ramona, hugging her tight, while sobs shook her shoulders. Then Abe and Ruth Masterson arrived, and Tess released Ramona to let her run to them. There was mingled pain and joy on Tess's face as she watched the little girl hug the Mastersons, calling them Mommy and Daddy. Hoyt related the happenings that had led up to the rescue of Ramona.

Sage stepped close to Tess and Hoyt. "Are you going to take Ramona now that you have a home to raise her in?"

Tess sighed and shook her head. "Abe and Ruth are wonderful parents. She belongs to them."

Sage nodded, suddenly feeling good inside. "You're a lucky man, Red," he said.

"What about Mr. Yake?" Ferris asked.

"Clem Yake isn't as unreasonable as he seems," Tess said. "Ufford was stirring him up. There'll be no more trouble now."

Sage didn't go to Ufford's funeral, nor did he go near Ferris' soddy during the week. He finished the ditch with the help of the homesteaders. Ferris came out several times, and Sage marveled at the quick recovery he had made from the shock of Ufford's treachery.

On Sunday afternoon he rode down to the TS to see Hoyt and found Debbie there with Tess. When Debbie started home, Sage mounted and splashed across the creek with her.

"Mind if I ride a way with you?"

She smiled. "I'd be glad to have you. Daddy has been expecting you to come down all week."

"I didn't think he'd want to see me after the trouble I started on Sunday."

"He wanted to thank you for that. And I do, too."

Her voice was low and her face was turned away. Sage looked at her in admiration. She and her father had had the world knocked out from under them, but they had come back, chins up, their faith still intact.

"I've got to hand it to you and your Dad, Debbie, for the way you've come through this last week."

"Neither man nor anything man-made can be depended on completely," she said, her voice tight. "It's in times like this that we have to have a greater power to reach up to."

Sage sighed. "You must have had something to reach up to. Still, I like to see what I believe in. Your Dad's faith is sometimes blind."

She nodded. "I know. But that same faith takes him through times like last week. You believe in what you can do for yourself. And that saved Daddy and me from a terrible mistake. It takes both kinds of faith, Sage."

"You may be right, Debbie. You placed a barrier between us once because we put our trust in different things. Will that always be there?"

"I don't think it was ever as big as I made it sound. I guess, like Daddy's, my faith too was blind."

"Maybe. But after watching you and your Dad this week, I think I have a little of that faith now."

"I'm glad. And my faith will never be blind again. Faith was meant to be strong but never blind."

"And that barrier?"

"It's gone, Sage. I can see lots of things I couldn't before."

"You know how I feel about you Debbie," he said, reaching over and taking her hand. "Don't encourage me too much or you'll have a hard time keeping me away."

"No one will ever keep you away, Sage."

They rode on in silence, but it was a rosy silence for Sage. Eden Valley was going to be the paradise its name suggested. The promise was there in the black eyes of the girl beside him.

The autumn afternoon faded into a golden twilight as the horses, unguided, made their way slowly toward the little cluster of homesteads.